STUCK WITH YOU

TITLES BY MEGAN BYRD

Take a Chance on Me

One Sweet Love

Merry & Brett

Stuck With You

MEGAN BYRD

Donna,
Enjoy life's adventures!

Megan Byrd

ARDENVILLE PRESS

For questions or inquiries: megan@meganbyrd.net

To Dad,
who's always up for an adventure.
I love you, too.

1

Abbie

MARCUS ENTERED THE PORTAL. This is the all-caps subject line for three dozen new emails that weren't in my inbox when I left the house thirty minutes ago. People outside my line of work might think about inter-dimensional travel, but I know it's just another day in college sports. Our top player decided he wanted to leverage the team's conference championship win and NCAA tournament appearance this season to get himself on a bigger Division 1 basketball team. I can't blame him for wanting to be on a team whose games are regularly shown on national television and can give him more NIL money. That's how it is these days. The news doesn't surprise me, but my boss is obviously freaking out.

Will Brentley, the Athletic Director here at UNC Asheville, hasn't been my biggest fan for the two seasons I've been with the program. If he knew Marcus Cobb had talked to me about his decision and that I'd encouraged him to do what he thought was best for himself, he'd probably blow a gasket. Maybe even work harder to get rid of me. Not that he has any valid reasons to do so. I've had the feeling since the first time we met that he's not a fan of a woman being the men's basketball team athletic trainer. Or maybe I'm reading more into his icy demeanor than is actually there. He could just be someone who doesn't like to mix work and friendship, but I think it's more than that.

Reading through the emails in the order he sent them, I realize they're all knee-jerk reactions to the announcement. The rest of our team is staying and we have some incoming freshman who will be assets. Losing one player, even if he is our top scorer, will not devastate the team. We have a brilliant coach who excels at honing players' strengths and gelling the team. The most recent email requests my presence in his office as soon as possible. I sigh, thinking about my agenda for the day. I have several appointments to schedule for players, a stack of notes to input into my computer from yesterday, and I need to prepare for the players who will be in to see me after lunch for treatment. Thankfully, we're in the brief lull between the end of the season and summer training, so my to-do list isn't longer.

I reply to the last email saying I'll be up to his office in ten minutes. My phone rings immediately.

"Abbie Price," I say, already knowing who's on the other line.

"Abigail," Will says, "I said ASAP. What's so important that you need ten minutes?"

I roll my eyes. No matter how many times I've asked him to call me Abbie, he still insists on using my given name. Not even my parents call me Abigail. "I'll be right up."

He hangs up without another word and I set down the receiver. I love everything about this job except my boss. The AD I worked under at Charleston was much more approachable. He gave me free rein to do my job and welcomed my thoughts when I had suggestions or concerns. Sometimes I wonder why I'm tolerating my current boss. Deep down, I know the answer is the closer proximity to my family, but on days like this, I question whether geographical closeness is more important than my mental health.

It really has been great being in the same city as my twin, Rachel. And Paul, our older brother, is just an hour's drive away. Hypothetically, it means I get to see my nieces on more than just holidays, but with the crazy schedule that comes with being part of college basketball, there have been years when I'm on the other side of the country at Thanksgiving because the team is playing in a tournament. My boss thinks my life needs to revolve around the UNCA men's basketball team and it does, though that means I barely have a social life. I haven't dated anyone seriously in years. It hasn't really been a priority, but I can admit to a few stirrings of longing from seeing my sister so in love. I wouldn't mind having someone to vent to when I have a crappy day or to go hiking with when I need to get out and work off some pent up energy. Alas, I've hardly explored my new city despite having been here for nearly two years.

I tap on Will's closed door, opening it when I hear him respond.

"What's up?"

He gives me an exasperated look. "Did you read *any* of my emails?"

"I read them all. There's nothing we can do about a player's decision to seek opportunities elsewhere."

He harrumphs. "Be that as it may, I can't understand why you don't seem shocked." He narrows his eyes. "Did you know about this?" His eyes round as a new thought enters his brain. "Did you *tell* Marcus to do it?"

I scowl at the accusation. "No, I didn't tell one of our players to leave the team. You think he'd listen to me, anyway?"

"Yeah, you're right," he says, waving away his accusation.

I only said that because I know he sees me as a glorified first-aid provider. Will hasn't ever taken me seriously despite the fact that I've done an excellent job keeping our team healthy and rehabbing the players who've dealt with injuries during the season. And the guys *do* talk to me. Not just about basketball, but other life stresses. I'm the guys' unofficial therapist, in addition to medical support. And I'm great at my job, even if my boss will never acknowledge it.

"Is there anything else you need to discuss?" I have something on my mind, but I want to make sure Will's more rational before bringing it up.

"Do you think anyone else will leave?"

I shake my head. "I doubt it. Tony and Brandon like how much playing time they got this year. Though I bet they're watching to see what happens with Marcus. If a school from one of the major conferences picks him up, they might make their move next season."

Will closes his eyes and rubs his temples. "Let's hope for our sake that doesn't happen."

Keeping my face neutral, despite how much I want to respond to his last comment, I take a breath before plunging forward. "Boss, have you looked at my proposal?"

"What proposal?"

"The one about hosting a summer clinic for high school students interested in sports medicine."

He opens his eyes, but focuses on his computer monitor rather than looking at me. "Oh, uh, I've glanced at it. Reach out late next week. I should have a chance to get through it by then. What kinds of resources would you need? Would it take away from your commitment to the team?"

Internally, I'm rolling my eyes, but showing my exasperation will not help my cause. "I've outlined everything in my proposal. Part of the clinic would be the students watching me work with the basketball team so they can really get a good feel for the job. Plus, when I ran the program in Charleston, several students decided to go to college there. It could be a good recruiting tool for the school."

He frowns and my heart sinks. He's never going to approve it, even with the evidence of how successful it's been. I probably should have given up after he shot it down last summer, but I thought perhaps with another year of stellar job performance, he might be more open to it. Maybe this isn't the place for me. But where else can I work close to family? Charlotte, maybe? They have an NBA team. What if I tried to break into the pros? I make a mental note to check out other colleges near here, as well as the professional team tonight after work.

"Check in with me next Friday."

That's definitely a 'no.' "Anything else?"

"You can go."

He still hasn't looked away from his computer screen. I get up, close the door behind me, and head back to my office. I'm tempted to let the interaction derail my day, but that wouldn't be fair to the students I'll be seeing later. In my office, I shake out my shoulders and punch the air a few times to get rid of my frustration. I really should put up a punching bag so I can get an actual workout in while working off some steam. Or I could just go over to the gym and use the one there on my break. Sitting back down at my computer, I give my head a hard shake to let go of my frustration from the meeting, and dive into work.

The rest of my day goes much better than the morning. I enjoy horsing around with players while I tape ankles and prod knees. The guys are in a pretty good mood, despite the news about Marcus. I'm sure he told everyone before the public announcement because that's the kind of guy he is. He'll definitely be missed, but there are plenty of talented players ready to take his place. Spending time with the students reminds me why I enjoy working here.

On the way home, I consider whether I could talk to someone else at the school about trying out my sports medicine clinic. Suddenly, my car jerks a few times and then the engine dies.

"No, no, no, no, no."

I steer it over to the shoulder and put it in park, a burning smell permeating my nose. That can't be good. I give it a minute, praying silently that the engine will start up and I can make it the remaining two miles home. Sucking in a deep breath, I press the brake and turn the key. "Come on, Susie, you can do it."

Nothing. I give it another minute, then try again. Still no luck. I drop my head to the steering wheel, defeated. So much for my day turning around.

Forty-five minutes later, I'm sitting in a hard plastic chair waiting for someone to tell me what's wrong with Susie. Having already forked out money for the tow truck, I am not looking forward to finding out how much it's going to cost for repairs. Even the radio in the shop blasting some of my favorite songs isn't making me feel better.

Finally, a guy in blue coveralls comes out from the garage.

"Blue Wrangler?"

I raise my hand and he saunters over, wiping his hands on a rag that used to be red.

"What's the diagnosis?" I say.

"You need a new transmission."

My shoulders slump. "That doesn't sound cheap."

He shakes his head. "As old as your car is, you'd be better off selling it for scrap and buying something newer."

That is not what I want to hear. "How much would it cost to replace the transmission?"

"About four thousand."

My eyes nearly pop out of my head. It doesn't seem smart to pump that much money into a twenty-year-old vehicle. "How would I sell it?"

"You can take it to the junkyard. Or we'll buy it for five hundred."

That's not a lot of money, but it's probably more than I'd make after paying for a tow truck to haul it somewhere else. Faced with two terrible options, I'm too beaten down by the day to exert much energy. "Yeah, okay. Five hundred is great."

"You need a box to clean out the interior?"

I blink, processing his words. Oh yeah. I'm not taking Susie home.

"That would be great, thanks."

After emptying my faithful ride, saying a proper goodbye to her, and calling a ride, I sit back down in one of the plastic chairs, the box resting on my lap. What am I going to do? I don't have a lot of savings because the cost of living in Asheville is higher than I'm used to. It seems like money is the answer to my current predicament, but college ATs don't rake in the dough and I don't know of any other prospects at the moment. I love what I do, so there's no question about looking for another profession.

To distract myself from my sorry state, I think about my schedule for tomorrow. Since it's nearly the end of the semester, the players are wrapping up their classes. Several players plan to stay on campus, take summer classes, and help Coach Maylor with his summer camp. I need to get a final headcount so I know who to check on the next few months. I consider a few more exercises to show Julian so he can strengthen the ankle he sprained in the last game of the season. Not wanting to forget them, I type myself a note on my phone.

This reminds me I'm now in need of transportation to work tomorrow. It'd cost too much for a ride share. The bus is more economical than a rental, but will take significantly longer. Technically, I could call my sister and see if I could borrow one of her family's cars, but I don't want to be a bother.

"Are you a fan of the Amazing Race television show?" I perk up. *Uh, yeah. That show is awesome!*

Looking around for the source of the voice, I realize it's a commercial playing over the radio.

"Have you ever thought about being a contestant?" *Only a thousand times.*

"This may be your lucky day!" *Tell me more.*

"The Asheville Chamber of Commerce is hosting its own Amazing Asheville competition in a few weeks." *I'm very intrigued. Keep going.*

"The competition will be a two-day race around the city to help promote tourism. The winners will receive fifty-thousand dollars and be the new spokespeople for Asheville tourism."

My mouth hangs open. *Fifty-thousand dollars?!* That would certainly be enough to replace Susie. And give me a little emergency savings so I won't have to sweat the small stuff so much. Money aside, though, how cool would it be to take part in an event like this? I've always wondered how I'd fare if I had a chance, but I don't know who can be my plus-one. I always imagined doing the race with my sister, but she's hard at work trying to meet her publisher's deadline, so she's probably out. I wonder if you have to have a partner or can do it solo?

I blink back to the present and realize I missed the last part of the commercial, which probably gave those kinds of details along with the registration information. I open a browser window on my phone to search for the contest, but am derailed by a notification that my ride has arrived. I climb into the back of a silver Subaru, smile at the man wearing a blue baseball cap, then search for the competition. I find the details on the Chamber's website. Teams of two for the competition, but the organizers will partner up solo participants.

I like the idea of something fun like this. There's one minor hitch, though. I'm not well versed in Asheville locations or history, so I don't know how good I'll be if there's any trivia involved. However, contestants in the Amazing Race go all over the world to places they don't know and mostly do fine. I'm usually pretty good at figuring things out. It'll be fine, I'm sure of it.

2

Carlos

I TAKE ONE last look around the room before shutting off the lights. TGIF. This week was nuts. Of course, clay week is always crazy. Trying to manage twenty-five classes of kids ranging from five to ten years of age is hard enough on a regular day. Arm them with balls of clay, cups of water, and etching tools, and all manner of things can go wrong. But there's no way I'll ever cut this plan of instruction. I love seeing what the kids come up with.

Each grade has an assigned project to keep things from going completely off the rails, but it still leaves plenty of room for individual creativity. I'm not sure which of the projects is my favorite—necklace pendants for kindergarten, snails for first-graders, owls for second-grade, coil pots for third, or masks for fourth.

All the projects are drying on the stage in the gym and will be ready to paint the week after next. I've prepared the students in advance that we won't be painting the pottery next week, but I'm sure they'll forget. I'm not a newbie after all. Next week we'll complete paint blots to help them remember color mixing and maybe make some butterflies.

Out at my car, I take a minute to let my head fall back against the headrest. I'm excited about the weekend. My family's having their first backyard party of the year. They usually start earlier, but we had a freak snow a few weeks ago, and the weather has only recently returned to normal temps.

We're not officially celebrating anything but, like my abuela says, just being together is all we need for a party. If it means getting to stuff myself full on pasteles, then I'm in. My buddy Jayson will be there with his wife. I'm so glad those two worked out their issues and found their happily ever after. Of course, now they've ganged up to find someone for me. Apparently, I'm not living my best life if I'm not also in love. But, whatever. I don't need a relationship to be happy. Besides, most of my free time is already spoken for.

When I'm not teaching art to the students at W. B. Hines Elementary School, I'm trying to make creations for Double Rainbow Designs, my fledgling art studio. I rent a space in the River Arts District and make all kinds of things—paintings, mixed-media sculptures, jewelry, and pottery. I've even dabbled in blown glass. I haven't yet found my niche, so I try a little of everything, hoping something will be a hit with potential buyers.

Ideally, I'd like to make art full-time, but that requires making enough money selling my art to afford my apartment, studio and gallery spaces, and essentials like gas, food, and electricity. Maybe one day.

My mind locks onto an idea for a sculpture, and I drive over to my studio on autopilot. It's nearly midnight when I step back and can't help but smile at the mountain landscape that emerged from the bundle of wire I held in my hands just hours ago. I'd like to paint it, but I'll do a better job after a night's rest. I grab a bottle of water out of the mini fridge and some crackers and a granola bar from the basket on top. Another gourmet dinner. Hey, at least I'm saving money somewhere. I'm just leaving room for all the great food tomorrow. Or maybe trying to fulfill the starving-artist trope. I honestly wouldn't mind breaking that mold.

I drive home and drag myself into bed, tired but satisfied. I made something good tonight. The smile is still on my lips when I fall asleep.

3

Abbie

I RESEARCHED BUS routes and found one half a mile from my house that goes to the university, so that was my mode of transportation today. It required leaving my house an hour earlier than normal this morning and walking in my front door after dark. Thank goodness it's Friday and I have a few days to figure out another way to get to and from work reliably. I don't like the options I've found so far.

My phone rings and Rachel's face pops up. "We're downstairs," she says when I answer.

"I'll be right down."

I grab my sling pack and head out front. I climb into the back of my sister's car since Julie, her sister-in-law, is occupying the passenger seat.

"Hey ladies."

"Hey Abs," Rachel says, but her smile drops when she sees

my hang dog expression. "What's wrong?"

"Let's get to wherever we're going and I'll fill you in."

"Sure thing. Julie and I thought B4 would be good. Is that okay?"

A big, juicy cheeseburger from Big Bob's Burger Barn sounds amazing right now. "It's perfect."

Julie and Rachel chat all the way to the restaurant while I zone in and out, trying to come up with a transportation solution that doesn't leave me broke by the end.

"Okay, spill," Rachel says, when we're seated in a booth and have drinks in front of us.

I sigh, take a drink of my soda, and share my woes. "I can't afford to buy a replacement vehicle at the moment and the bus schedule is not ideal for getting me to work when I need to. Plus, it isn't as punctual as I'd like it. But, as far as I can tell, it's really my only option."

"Wow, that *is* a lot," says Julie. "I'm really sorry, Abbie."

I give her a small smile. "Thanks."

Rachel's forehead creases in thought. "Tom and I could loan you money if you'd like."

My nose wrinkles. "No, thanks. That's very generous of you, but I don't want to have a loan between us. It'd be too awkward. Anyway, enough about me. Let's hear about you two. What's going on?"

Rachel hesitates, sisterly concern obvious on her face, but after a pointed look from me, her frown turns up into a smile. "I almost have a complete draft of the book. My editor's read the first half and thinks it's great."

"That's awesome, Rach. Congrats!"

"Thanks. I'm hoping to write the next book in the series by the end of the year."

"Two books in one year? That seems like a lot."

"Yeah," Julie says. "What's the rush?"

Rachel's eyes sparkle. "I'd like to complete my current contract before the baby comes."

"You're pregnant?!" Julie and I screech in unison.

"I'm pregnant!"

I slide out of my side of the booth and Julie and I squeeze Rachel together in a hug sandwich.

"I'm going to be an aunt!"

"Me too," says Julie.

Rachel shakes her head at me. "You're already an aunt, you goober."

I grin. "Oh yeah. You're right."

Julie refocuses the conversation. "When are you due?"

"November fourth."

"So exciting!"

"It is. So, tell us how married life is going."

Julie's smile widens. "It's fantastic. Well, except for getting used to sharing a closet with another person. Jayson's suits take up more room than I expected."

Rachel chuckles. "We all have to make sacrifices, but it's worth it."

I'm happy for both of them, but there's a twinge of envy in my gut. Rachel must sense my stilted emotion because she gives me a sympathetic look, which annoys me. Sure, things are a bit rough at the moment, but I'll figure it out. I always do. I know how to set and achieve goals and won't let anything stop me. This is just a small stumbling block on the road to success. The thought reminds me of the one good thing to come out of this week.

"I do have something kind of exciting to share."

Rachel perks up. "What is it?"

"The Chamber of Commerce is holding a competition kind of like the Amazing Race to find their newest tourism spokespeople. I filled out an application earlier in the week and received an email today that I've been accepted."

"That's really cool," Julie says. "Do you have a teammate?"

"Not yet, but I will. Single contestants will be paired up with one another." I look at Rachel. "I thought about asking if you wanted to do it with me, but figured you'd be busy. Now that I know you're pregnant, I think I made a wise decision."

"You're right. I've been pretty exhausted lately. There's no way I'd have the energy needed. When does the race take place?"

"In a couple of weeks. It's only a two-day event, held over the weekend, which works out with my schedule."

"What do the winners get?"

"They get to be the face of Asheville Tourism and make some television ads. They also receive fifty-thousand dollars."

Julie whistles. "That'd solve your car troubles."

"You're telling me. I'd only get half, but that can get me a very nice used car."

"I bet this is something Tom would love to do," Rachel says, "but unfortunately, he'll just be getting back from Australia and the jet lag is a beast."

"I thought he was scaling back on work commitments."

"He is, but because I'm pregnant, we negotiated and agreed that he'd take on assignments now and then stay home after the baby's born."

"That makes sense."

"Yeah. Besides, I can spend as much time as I want writing and not feel like I'm ignoring him."

"What about work?"

Rachel smiles. "I'm going to talk to Sarah on Monday about

that. I'll want to stay home for a while after the baby's born and then maybe only work part-time when Tom's around."

"That's cool."

"Oh! Abs, you can use Tom's car until you get yours fixed."

"Um..."

"It's perfect! Tom's headed out of town Sunday afternoon. We won't need it, and you'll have reliable transportation."

It would provide a temporary fix to my dilemma. "Are you sure?"

"Yeah, of course. No problem."

"Thanks. I'd love to borrow it while he's gone."

Rachel nods decisively. "Great."

Our food arrives and we dig in. The first bite of my cheeseburger is heavenly.

"Do either of you have any plans this weekend?" I ask.

Julie holds up a finger and finishes chewing. "Tomorrow we're all going to a party. You should come with us!"

"Where is it?"

"One of Jayson's friends is hosting. I've been before and the food is amazing. It's so much fun."

"It'll be my first time going." Rachel's eyes plead with me to accept. "We can be newbies together."

I know how much she hates being in a crowd of strangers. I didn't have any other plans, and I definitely owe Rachel for letting me use Tom's car. "Yeah, okay."

"Great! We'll pick you up around noon. You can drop us off after and then take Tom's car home with you."

"Sounds like a plan."

Tom's SUV pulls up to the curb where I'm standing in front of my apartment building. I slide into the back seat and set the Tupperware container I'm holding down next to me.

Rachel turns around in her seat. "What did you bring?"

"I made some cookies. Didn't want to show up empty-handed."

"That's sweet, but the way Julie talks, there's going to be more than enough food."

I shrug. "I doubt anyone will mind extra dessert."

"I certainly won't," Tom says from the driver's seat.

"Thanks for letting me borrow your car."

"No prob. We're family. We help each other, right?"

I suppose that's true, though I've never been very good at accepting help. But I'll return the car with a full tank, freshly washed, and vacuumed until its spotless. And maybe offer free babysitting when the nibling arrives.

"Congrats on the baby, too. Very exciting."

Tom grins. "Thanks. I'm thrilled." He places a hand on his wife's flat abdomen.

Rachel shakes her head. "He's already talking about how cute I'll be when I have a true baby bump."

"I'm sure your parents are excited for their first grandchild," I say to Tom.

"We haven't told them yet. We're going to fly out when I get back from Australia and tell them in person."

"Does that mean our parents don't know yet?"

Rachel shakes her head. "We're trying to figure out when we can see them as well."

"They'll be in Greenville for Natalie's kindergarten graduation."

"Oh yeah, I forgot about that. But I don't want to take away from Nat's big day."

"I'm sure it'll be fine."

Tom pulls over to the side of the road and parks behind another car. "We're here."

When I get out, I'm shocked by the amount of cars parked along the street. "Whoa."

"Whoa is right," Rachel says. "I didn't think the party was this big."

I pull her into a side hug. "It'll be fine."

We make our way to the front door and Tom rings the bell. The door opens and a man with silver and black speckled hair and tan skin looks at us expectantly.

"Hi, I'm Tom Haynes. This is Rachel and Abbie. My sister Julie and her husband, Jayson, invited us."

"Oh, one of Jayson's friends. Bienvenidos. Come on in." He ushers us into the foyer. "I'm Javier. Please make yourself at home. Drinks are on the deck out back and the food is getting set up on tables in the yard."

"Thank you," Tom says. We walk through the house to the backyard.

There's a woman arranging dishes on the table, and I carry my cookies over to her. "Hi, I'm Abbie. I brought cookies."

The woman smiles. "Hola, hija. You can set them down on the end of the table."

"Everything looks and smells amazing, Mrs…"

"Thank you. Call me Veronica. When you're in our home, you're family."

"Okay, Veronica."

I set the cookies down with the other desserts and look around for Rachel and Tom. I see them in a group with Julie and Jayson. Standing with his back to me is a guy of average height with short black hair and tan skin. He's wearing jeans and a T-shirt that flatters him well. His arms are well-defined and I take a moment to appreciate them. He turns his head slightly and flashes a smile of straight, white teeth. I feel drawn toward him and make my way across the grass to the group.

Rachel is the first to notice me and puts an arm around my shoulder. "Hey, Abbie. I just ran into a blast from the past. Remember this guy from high school? It's his parents' house."

My gaze lasers in on who I thought was a handsome stranger. My eyes narrow and, if I could shoot fire from them, I would. His name leaves my mouth as a growl. "Carlos Vega."

4

Carlos

MY EYES SNAP over to a familiar face and my breath catches. It's Abbie Price. I'm not sure why she spoke my name so menacingly, but there's no time to ask as she spins on her heels and marches away from the group. I look at her sister for an explanation. She gives an apologetic shrug and turns to follow Abbie.

"Don't mind her," Julie says, patting my arm. "She's had a rough week."

"What happened?"

Julie waves her hand. "Transportation issues."

A pang of concern hits me in the chest. I hate to see someone struggling. "Is it anything I can help with?"

Julie smiles. "You're sweet, but I don't think so."

"Is Abbie in town for a visit?"

"She moved up here a while ago."

This piques my interest. "Oh, yeah?"

Julie nods. "She's the basketball athletic trainer over at UNC Asheville."

"That's cool."

Jayson leans in to our conversation. "Jules, tell Carlos about the competition Abbie's doing." He looks at me. "It seems right up your alley."

Jayson knows I love doing crazy races and activities. I don't know of anything happening in the next couple of months, so I'm intrigued.

"Oh, yeah!" Julie says. "The city is holding a two-day scavenger hunt type race to find their new tourism spokespeople. It'll be teams of two, and the winners get fifty-thousand dollars."

Whoa. Fifty-thousand dollars? I could do a lot with that. Though I guess it's actually half of that with a partner. Still, that would help with materials and rent. It could help me get closer to my goal of working full time on my art.

"That sounds pretty cool. How do I sign up?"

"Visit the Chamber of Commerce website. Everything's on there."

A thought wriggles inside my brain. "Does Abbie have a teammate already?"

"She signed up as an individual, but the organizers will pair up any individuals they accept."

"Okay, cool."

Jayson slaps a hand on my shoulder. "You're going to apply, right?"

I grin. "You know I am."

I look around the yard and notice Abbie and Rachel having a very animated conversation. I'm not sure what's being said, but

Abbie doesn't look happy. She nods and Rachel pulls her into a hug. My eyes follow them over to the line of coolers on the deck. Suddenly, I'm feeling quite parched.

"I'm going to grab a soda. Do either of you want anything?"

"Nah, I'm good," says Jayson.

"I'd love a water," says Julie.

"Coming right up."

I walk across the yard to the coolers. I find Julie a water and grab a Sprite for myself. Abbie is just a few feet away. Time for a proper introduction. I step up next to her. "Hey—"

I'm interrupted by a piercing whistle. All eyes turn toward my father. He grins. "Gracias por venir. La comida está lista. Disfrútenla."

I look back over toward Abbie, but she's disappeared. I look around but don't see her anywhere. Rachel is back beside Tom, so I head her way, pausing only to give Julie a bottle of water.

"Hey, Rachel. Where's Abbie?"

"She's around here somewhere."

"Is she okay?"

Rachel sighs and rolls her eyes. "Yes. She's just being Abbie."

I'm not exactly sure what that means, but I nod anyway.

"I heard she moved here for work."

"That's right."

"Is it nice having her close by again?"

She smiles, but then her forehead crinkles. "It is, but I'm concerned for her."

"Why's that?"

"She's having a rough time at the moment. It's expensive enough living here, but she's been having car issues and her boss is making work a bit of a struggle."

I feel my inner protector stirring. However, I doubt Abbie

would welcome any help I offered. She was fiercely independent in high school and I doubt much has changed. "That sounds tough."

Rachel nods. "Yeah, it is. It's nice to see your family again. I hear one of your sisters recently got married."

"Yes, Angelica. James is a great guy. I'm happy for them."

"That's wonderful."

I spot Abbie coming out of the house. "There's Abbie. I'll go say hi."

Rachel scrunches up her face. "That may not be the best idea."

"Why not?"

Rachel's face flushes. "She's still a little mad about senior prom."

Her comment intrigues me. "Is she mad I asked you to go?"

She furrows her forehead. "No. She's angry about you convincing Ryan Johnston not to take me."

I'm not quite following. "But that affected you. If anything, *you* should be the one mad at me."

"Oh, I know. And I was, but that was a long time ago. Besides, it's not like I was going to marry him or anything. But you know Abbie. She's fiercely loyal and considers anything done to me as a personal affront against her."

The last few weeks of high school suddenly make sense. "Is that why she stopped speaking to me?"

"Yes."

"And covered my car in shaving cream?"

"Yep."

"Is that also why she toilet papered the tree in our front yard?"

Rachel giggles and nods.

I shake my head, admiring her tenacity. "It took me two days to get all of it out of the branches. My dad was furious." My eyes widen. "Please don't tell him it was her. He still brings that up every once in a while."

"My lips are sealed."

"And you're saying she's still harboring a grudge against me?"

"Apparently so."

"Huh. Well, for what it's worth, I'm sorry I hurt you. That wasn't my intention."

Rachel smiles. "Eh, it was a small thing in the grand scheme of life, but I appreciate the apology." Her stomach growls and she chuckles. She waves toward the tables ladened with dishes. "I obviously need some of that delicious food over there."

"I'll join you. I could also use some pasteles in my belly."

5

Abbie

I STALK OVER to my sister, who's seated in a chair with a plate of food. "I can't believe you were talking to him."

Her innocent eyes meet mine. "Who?"

"Carlos."

Rachel shakes her head. "Abbie, let it go. That was ages ago."

"But he hurt you."

"It doesn't matter now. Besides, he apologized."

I scowl, not pleased that my sister let him off the hook for his horrid behavior.

She sighs. "It's not like we did nothing dumb in high school."

Nothing comes to mind right away. "Like what?"

"How about putting rainbow streaks in our hair right before picture day?"

"That was awesome, not dumb."

"Have you looked at our sophomore yearbook photos lately?

The look didn't age well."

I shrug. "Still, that was harmless. Other than annoying our parents, it didn't affect anyone else."

"What about when you ruined Sarah Dawson's project for the science fair freshman year?"

My eyes widen. I'd forgotten about that. "It was an accident. I didn't know the ball was going to hit her hydroponic garden."

"Intentions don't wipe out consequences, unfortunately."

My ire deflates in the face of Rachel's poignant words. I felt awful about what happened to Sarah's amazing garden. It must have taken her months of work and I'd destroyed her chances of winning the trip to Space Camp that went to the winner of the fair. I apologized, but couldn't fix what I had broken. We weren't friends after that and I couldn't blame her.

Okay, so maybe I'm not perfect, but messing with my family is always going to put someone on my bad side. I see nothing wrong with that. But perhaps there's a time and place to let go. Though, that doesn't have to be right now, does it?

"I see your point," I say, ready to move on to a more comfortable topic. My stomach grumbles.

"Go get some food," Rachel says, "and come keep me company. I don't know many people here."

"Fine. I'll be back."

I glance around to make sure Carlos isn't close by. Not seeing him anywhere, I walk over to the table and fill a plate. I don't know what some dishes are, but they smell amazing, so I take a little of everything, then pick up a folding chair and carry it over to where Rachel is under a tree.

"Good idea finding shade."

"I know. It's getting surprisingly warm for April."

"I'm impressed this food isn't bothering your stomach. Aren't you supposed to be nauseous right now?"

Rachel lifts a shoulder. "I haven't had any problems yet. Maybe I'll be one of the lucky ones and skip morning sickness."

"I hope so."

"This rice is amazing. Have you tried it yet?"

I stick a forkful in my mouth and close my eyes as the flavor explodes in my mouth. "You're right."

"I think I love Puerto Rican food. We should go visit sometime."

"That'd be fun. If I win Amazing Asheville, I can afford a ticket and we can go, maybe before you get too far along?"

"That'd be great. But you know we could go, anyway. Tom's got tons of airline miles so we could get free tickets. Then we just have to split a hotel."

I shake my head. "No, that's okay. It'll give me extra motivation to win."

"But even if you don't win—"

I glare at her, and she holds up a hand to keep me from speaking.

"And you probably will, but even if not, I still want to go. We haven't traveled together since freshman year of college. It'll be like a babymoon but for sisters. A sistermoon!"

I groan. "That's not a thing." Her words remind me we stopped taking trips together when she started dating that creep, Chris. At least she finally found a decent guy. Not that I didn't have my doubts about Tom for a while. But he straightened up, and it's obvious to everyone how in love they are.

"Well, it should be," Rachel says, breaking into my thoughts.

"Okay, let's make it happen, then."

"Excellent! Send me available dates and I'll start planning."

"I'll look at my schedule this week."

"Will you do me one more favor?"

The pleading look in her eye makes me wary. It's the look she usually has when she knows I won't like what she has to say.

"What?"

"Will you at least say hi to Carlos? We are at his family's party, after all."

I tip my head back and close my eyes. *Lord, give me strength.* "Fine," I hiss. "But just for you. Not for him."

Rachel smiles sweetly at me and squeezes my arm. "Thanks, sis. You're the best."

I look around and see him at the food table. I stand up and take a step.

"While you're there, will you get me some dessert?"

I look back at my sister, and she bats her eyelashes at me. I grin at her theatrics. "Sure thing, little sis."

It feels like a death march to the table. I have to will each leg to take a step closer to the man I've hated for so many years. Pretending like I don't see him, I veer over to the end with the desserts. I'd rather he not know my true purpose for coming to the table. I grab a plate and add a few things, not sure what Rachel might like the most.

"I don't remember you having such a sweet tooth."

I close my eyes to brace myself before opening them and fixing a smile on my lips. "I don't. This is for Rachel."

"Ah, of course. She definitely does. One of the many differences between the two of you."

What does that mean? I don't have time to form a rebuttal because he keeps talking.

"Hi, by the way. I'm quite surprised to see you."

"I could say the same thing."

He grins, and it pains me to notice anew how attractive he is.

Even more so this close up.

"I was also surprised to see Rachel. Jayson said he was bringing some friends, but I didn't realize I'd know them."

I don't know what to say to that. "The food's great. I'd love to thank the cook."

"That would be my mom. She's over there." He points to a group of people laughing. "She's the one in the blue and green shirt."

I purse my lips. "You mean the only woman?"

Carlos smiles. "Yeah, I suppose that would have worked, too."

I feel like I've done my duty. I'll thank Carlos's mom and I can continue ignoring him for the rest of my life. "Okay, bye."

"Hey, I heard you live here now."

Why won't he let me leave? Did he believe I really thought it was good to see him? Be polite, Abbie. This is Rachel's friend, apparently. "Yep." The word comes out clipped. So much for politeness, though it doesn't seem to bother him.

"I love it here. Lots of gorgeous hikes and scenic views. There's always something to do."

I don't remember Carlos having an interest in the outdoors. He was athletic because he played basketball, but I don't remember hiking being his thing. Perhaps he's yanking my chain. I can't help but find out if he's lying. "What's the best hike you've done?"

"It depends on the time of year. Looking Glass Rock is awesome in the fall when the leaves are turning brilliant hues of red, orange, and yellow. Courthouse Creek has an awesome waterfall and pool for swimming, though it's not very strenuous. Rainbow Falls is also gorgeous, especially on a sunny day." He chuckles. "Can you tell I like waterfalls?"

I mentally jot those down. I'll have to check them out

sometime. "Thanks for the recommendations."

"If you ever need a hiking buddy, let me know. I'd be happy to go with you."

Like I'd ever volunteer to spend time with him. "Good to know. I'd better get this plate to Rachel."

"Yeah, sure thing. It's so great to see you, Abbie."

I tip my chin up in acknowledgement, unable to respond in kind. I feel a little guilty for being rude. Carlos seems to want to be friends, but I can't forget the past. When I reach Rachel, I hand her the plate and sit back down.

Rachel nudges my shoulder. "So?"

"What?"

"How'd it go?"

"Fine."

"He's nice, right?"

"I guess."

"And he's become quite a looker, too."

"A *looker*? Are you eighty years old?"

She shrugs. "I must be spending too much time with Louise. She's always saying cute things like that."

I'm done with this conversation and stand up. "I'm going to go thank Carlos's mom for the great food."

"Ooh, I'll come with you. Maybe I can convince her to share her rice recipe."

6

Carlos

JAYSON AND I jump up from the couch with simultaneous shouts of excitement, slapping our hands together in a high five after a player dunks the ball. We've made it a habit of watching at least one professional basketball game together each week. Basketball's always been a good connection point for us. We played against each other in high school and now we're on a recreational league together, the Ball-Stars. Jayson joined my team when he moved up here. Our league's currently over until the summer session starts up.

I thumb through my phone during commercials. My notifications show a new email, so I open it. I skim the message and grin. "Alright!"

Jayson's head snaps up from his phone to the television. "What? Did I miss another awesome dunk?"

"No. I've been accepted as a contestant for the Amazing

Asheville competition."

"Congratulations, 'Los! You're going to be awesome."

"Thanks." Looks like I'll be seeing Abbie again soon.

"When does it start?"

"There's an information session this Saturday for all the competitors, and then the actual event is the following weekend."

"Wow, that's quick."

"They probably want to get their spokespeople chosen and working before summer travel season starts."

"Oh yeah. Good point. Well, I think you have a great shot at winning."

"I appreciate it, man."

I settle into the couch as the game comes back on. The Hornets are beating the Pelicans by fifteen, but there's still plenty of time left. Seeming to prove my point, the Hornets are only up by six at the next time out.

Jayson groans. "These guys are killing me."

"You know you love the suspense."

He smiles. "True."

I have another new email and open it up. The news is even better than the previous one.

"Hey, Jay, guess what? One of my sculpture pieces sold."

"Wow, this is your night!"

"I know. And get this. They want to commission me to make a second one."

"Dude, that's huge. Congratulations."

I keep reading and my heart sinks. "There's a big problem, though. They want it finished in two weeks."

"Is that not enough time?"

"The piece they bought took me two months to make."

"Yikes. Why do they want it so soon?"

"I don't know. If I didn't have to work, it might be doable, but that's not really an option."

"Could you take vacation time?"

"I used all mine up for our family trip to Puerto Rico over Christmas. I'll respond and see if I they can extend the deadline. It can't hurt to ask."

I type a reply and am surprised when there's a new email a few minutes later.

"It's an anniversary gift. They said if I can do it, they'll give me an extra thousand for the rush."

Jayson whistles. "They must really like what you make."

"I guess so."

"What are you going to do?"

"I'm gonna go for it. If I can please this customer, maybe they'll tell their friends about me. It could become a fantastic opportunity. But it means all my free time will be at the studio. I'm going to have to take a rain check on watching games until it's finished."

"I understand. Do what you need to do."

I appreciate Jayson's understanding and support. "Thanks, man."

I show up for the Amazing Asheville information session, exhausted. I've been busting my butt working on the new piece. The wire I'm working with has been causing me trouble, and I've had to start over several times. I didn't know commission work would be this stressful. When I'm just making something for fun, it doesn't matter what the end result is. But the customer will compare this piece with the other one and I want it to blow them away. I have to get it done before the competition starts next week, which means I only have six more days to work, five of which include my day job. Seven, if this doesn't take all day.

I'm grateful to see they've set up a table with coffee and pastries and beeline for the much-needed caffeine. I don't even bother to doctor it up, but toss back an entire cup of black coffee in one gulp, then fill my cup again before grabbing what looks to be a bear claw and taking a seat. There are a dozen other people here already, sitting together in pairs. I guess they came with teammates. Abbie's not here yet.

I eat the pastry and do my best to keep my eyes open. The scrape of a chair makes my head snap up and I realize I'd been dozing. Most of the chairs have filled up. There are a few people sitting alone like me, but most people already have partners.

I look closer at the singles, trying to see who I should pair up with. There's a man in workout shorts and a T-shirt who looks like he's ready to start the race right now. A woman in jeans and a blouse sits a few rows behind him. Her thin frame looks like that of a dancer. Her eyes narrow as she assesses the competition. There are two other men sitting alone but in the same row. They seem to be deep in conversation. *Probably agreeing to team up if that's allowed.* That's only five singles, including me. Abbie glides in through the door and my eyes are immediately glued to her. She's in a T-shirt and shorts, her hair in a ponytail.

She meets my gaze, and something like panic skitters across her face before her expression settles into displeasure. She breaks eye contact and chooses a seat in the front. I can't help but think it's because it's about as far away from me as she can get.

Could Abbie handle working together with me for several days? She certainly didn't hide her disdain for me at the party. I can't believe she's still mad about something that happened in high school—something that didn't even involve her. If I'd known she'd hate me for more than a decade, would I still do it? Probably.

A man and woman in slacks and dress shirts walk to the front of the room. The man scans the room, probably performing a head count, and nods to the woman. She claps her hands together twice and all conversations cease.

"Welcome to the Amazing Asheville race! You are our twenty lucky competitors vying for a chance to become the new spokespeople for Asheville tourism. I'm Shannon Turle and this is my colleague, Trey Mapes. We're representing the Chamber of Commerce. Thank you all for coming. We have a lot of information to cover, so please grab something to eat and drink and we'll get started in two minutes."

A few people visit the table, but conversation doesn't resume. There's a buzz of excited tension among those of us in the room.

Trey clears his throat. "Like Shannon said, we're here to find our new tourism representatives, and you twenty were chosen from over one thousand applications."

My eyes widen in surprise. I didn't realize there would be so many interested in competing. Though, I suppose, fifty-thousand dollars is quite an incentive. I feel quite lucky to have been one of those chosen. While the money would help, I also just love taking part in wacky and random events. I've done a Pi(e) Day run, a 3-point competition, and even a hot pepper eating contest. That one affected me for days, but I placed second and received a year's supply of hot sauce along with a shirt showing a chili pepper breathing out fire that says "It's never spicy enough for me," so it wasn't all bad.

"Some of you already know who your partner is, but for those of you singles, today's the day we pair you up. Let's go ahead and do that so that you can officially meet and get to know each other.

Maybe discuss strategy. Would you six come up, write your name on a piece of paper, and stick it in this glass bowl?"

I set my coffee down and go to the front of the room. When all the names are in what looks like a goldfish bowl, Shannon picks it up and swirls the names around. She pulls out two together and hands them to Trey.

"Our first pairing is…Jeremy and Todd."

The men who were already talking to one another smile and slap their hands together in an enthusiastic high-five. That now leaves my potential teammates as the ballerina, athletic shorts guy, or Abbie. I look furtively at Abbie and find her looking back at me. She looks away first.

"Our second pairing is Amanda and…"

Trey grins, apparently enjoying the opportunity to drag things out. "Steve!"

My eyes shoot to Abbie. Her face looks a little pale. Is she okay?

"So our last couple will be Abbie and Carlos. Congratulations everyone! Let's get on with rules and whatnot for the competition."

Abbie zooms back to her seat without a glance my way. I retrieve my coffee from the back and sit down next to her, my leg grazing hers. She scoots to her left so that there's a seat between us. This may turn out to be a terrible mistake.

7

Abbie

PANIC RACES THROUGH my veins. I've been paired up with Carlos? Out of one thousand applicants, how did *he* end up as my partner? I should have asked Rachel to do the competition with me after all. It may have been a challenge with her pregnancy, but we'd have made it fun. Of course, we might not have won.

Despite the fact that I will not enjoy having to work together with this man, I must acknowledge that we have a decent chance of winning. Especially because he's in excellent physical condition and, if his presence in all of my high school honors courses was any indication, he's smart, too. It pains me to admit that, but at least these concessions are in my head, so no one else knows these somewhat charitable thoughts I have toward Carlos.

The closeness of his body to mine in these tiny plastic chairs, even with a seat between us, makes me feel self-conscious of his presence. I don't remember him being taller than me. He definitely wasn't this muscular in high school. Rachel's reminder that people can change echoes in my head. I'll concede that he's definitely become a man in the physical sense, but I have serious doubts about whether his integrity and character have improved.

"You all will be given branded T-shirts to wear throughout the competition," Shannon says. "Each team will have their own color. You will be required to turn over your personal cell phones for the duration of the event, but will receive a competition phone to use for mapping your locations, taking photographs, making phone calls, and communicating with your event liaison."

I don't remember reading in the fine print about not being able to use my phone, but I can live without it. It's just two days. That's the mantra I need to keep repeating to myself now that I've been paired up with my least favorite person in the world. I cannot believe that I have to work with Carlos Vega. Just thinking his name in my head makes my blood boil. But, as much as I despise him, I could really use the cash prize.

Can I put away all the revulsion I feel for him as a person in exchange for a lot of money? I don't feel good about it. It feels like I'm sacrificing my integrity. Rachel says I should move on like she has, but it still feels like I'm betraying her. *Suck it up for two days and then you never have to see him again. Plus, you can get a new car.* Fine. I'll do it, but I don't have to like it. Besides, I'm good at trivia and escape rooms and scavenger hunts, so I doubt I'll need Carlos's help. I can act like a solo team and let him tag along.

I realize I've zoned out on whatever Shannon was saying. I tune back in.

"There will be nine events on the first day. Each team will have the same clues but in a different order except for the last one, which will be our rendezvous point. You will prove that you've reached each checkpoint by taking a photo of the location, item, or completed challenge, and texting it to your assigned liaison, who will then send the next clue. Some will require finding specific items or locations while others will be physical challenges. The first day of the competition will have nine clues. Teams who reach the rendezvous point by eleven-thirty p.m. will continue on to the second day. Day two will have eleven challenges, with the winners being the team that reaches the finish line first."

That sounds doable. I wonder if we'll get money for transportation, food, and water like in the real Amazing Race. I raise my hand.

The woman shakes her head. "We will take questions at the end."

Okay then. I drop my arm and glance over at Carlos, who's taking notes on his phone. Smart. I should probably do that as well. I bend down, unzip my bag, and pull out my phone, typing in my question before I forget it. Next, I type everything I remember Shannon saying along with what's now being said.

"The event will be held even if it rains, so plan accordingly. You can bring a backpack with anything you might need for a two-day race. We will provide you with a list of banned items and inspect your bags before the competition starts next week to make sure everyone is on a fair playing field."

That's good to know, though I don't know what I'll need other than water, snack bars, sunscreen, and maybe a change of clothes.

"Also, we will have some cameras that will film you during the competition. You signed your permission for this in your application. We may use some of it in our new advertisement campaign."

Shannon looks over at Trey. "I think that's it. Did I forget anything?"

"I don't think so."

"Alright, then we'll now take any questions you have."

"Do we get any money for food or transportation?"

I'm glad someone else has that question.

Trey sighs. "As you may recall from our discussion of your competition-issued phones, there will be credits on the car rider app and a prepaid card in the wallet for food or other incidentals."

I grimace. Guess I did miss a few important things. Maybe I can get Carlos to send me his notes. Not that I need his help. Just that it'd be good to start on the same page. I'll do it after the briefing.

After fifteen more minutes of Q and A, we're dismissed until next Saturday when we'll meet in Pack Square at seven a.m. for the competition.

I turn toward Carlos. "Hey, will you send me your notes?"

He nods at the phone in my hands. "Didn't you take your own?"

How do I play this? "I did, but, uh, my app crashed halfway through and I'm afraid I might have missed something. I'd like to be thoroughly prepared so we can win this thing."

"Yeah, okay. What's your number?"

I give it to him, keenly aware that my enemy can now contact me whenever he wants. Maybe I'll get a new number after this is over.

My phone buzzes. I open the text, save the notes in my phone, and add his number to my contacts as M.E.

"What's M.E. mean?"

Startled, I look up. Carlos is peering at my phone. It stands for My Enemy, but I don't want him to know that since I need us to be cordial next weekend. I rack my brain for something plausible and come up with a response that will make me look dumb, but not suspicious. "Mi emigo."

"Amigo starts with 'a'. Unless you mean 'enemigo.'"

"What's enemigo mean?"

"Enemy."

"Oh. Uh, no, the first one."

I change the contact to M.A. though in my heart it stays M.E. Enemigo for sure.

"Why don't you use my actual name?"

"I like to give my friends code names, so if my phone is ever stolen, no one knows who my contacts are."

"Paranoid much?"

I shrug. "I have contact info for the entire UNCA basketball team. Some of them may go pro one day. I like to respect their privacy."

"I suppose that's smart."

I'm dreading what I'm about to say, but if we're going to win, which is the goal, it's necessary to do some additional preparation together. "Should we get together before next Saturday to talk about strategy or something? What to pack in our bags?"

"We can just send texts. I don't think we have to meet again."

I'm surprised by this, but maybe he's received the not-so-subtle back-off signals I've been sending him. "Okay. Then I guess I'll see you next Saturday at seven."

"Sounds good."

Carlos is out of his chair and through the door before I can even say bye. I wonder if I should feel offended at his quick exit, but I suppose I should be happy he isn't eager to spend extra time with me, either. Guess he's gotten the message, but why does that make me feel a little guilty?

8

Carlos

I RUN UP the street, checking my phone every few seconds in case by some miracle time has stopped and I'm not actually running. But alas, time keeps moving and so do I, the buildings next to me passing in a blur, just like this entire week.

After the info session, I headed back to my studio to continue to work on the piece that was due yesterday. My poor students must have thought I was a zombie with the dark circles under my eyes and the mumbles and grunts I gave in response to questions. I scuttled my plans of weaving with paper and had them all draw a picture of them as adults in their career with at least six details and some color. The kindergarteners always have a few fun professional goals. This year, along with the usual teacher, firefighter, doctor, etc, there were three cats, two superheroes, and a Target employee.

I was pleasantly surprised yesterday when Principal Lipscomb wished me luck on the race over the loudspeaker. I suppose it is kind of a big deal, though I'm just excited about the challenge. And to get to spend some time with Abbie and maybe convince her I'm not really the evil guy she thinks I am.

Though if I don't make it to Pack Square on time, it won't help my case. I sprint the last few blocks and reach the tents where everyone is mingling at six fifty-nine. I put my hands on my knees and take a few deep breaths.

"Glad you could grace us with your presence."

Abbie's eyes look like they want to shred me into pieces. I stand up and give her what I hope is a winsome smile. "Just wanted to get your adrenaline pumping early so we'll be ready when we get our first clue."

She rolls her eyes. "Yeah, right. Where's your backpack?"

I groan and slap my forehead.

Abbie sighs dramatically. "Lucky for you, I expected this and brought an extra water bottle along with everything else you were supposed to pack."

I feel terrible, but it's not just because I let Abbie down. I slept through my first two alarms after a week of all-nighters at the studio. I managed to get the piece finished and delivered yesterday after school, but I crashed hard as soon as I got home. Luckily, I set four alarms just in case. The third one was set to "fire alarm blare," which is guaranteed to get me up and the fourth sounded like the warning horn on a submarine, which means get your rear in gear and move like there's a bear chasing you. I'd actually managed to get out of the house before that one, but I was still a ways away. Hence the running.

But despite getting a good ten hours of sleep, I am still exhausted and need more than adrenaline to help my brain function for the weekend. If Abbie is still as competitive and driven as she was in high school, then I need to be on my toes, because this is going to be serious.

"Thanks for saving my backside. I promise I'll be a better teammate once things begin."

"Uh huh." She looks skeptical, but she's stuck with me, so what can she do?

"Do you know if they have any coffee? Also, do you happen to have a granola bar or something? I didn't have time to eat."

"Coffee's over there, along with some food."

"Great, thanks. I'll be right back."

The first cup of coffee burns my throat going down, but it's worth it. I refill the cup and look over the food selection. There's fresh fruit, some snack bars, and doughnuts again.

"Okay, contestants. Gather round."

I turn and see Shannon and Trey in the next tent. I shove a few snacks in my pocket and grab an apple before heading their direction and taking my place next to Abbie. My first bite of apple makes a sharp crunch. Abbie winces and takes a step away from me. I wonder if she's one of those people who can't stand the sound of other people chewing. I try to eat the apple more quietly, turning my head away before taking bites.

"We're glad to see you all made it," Shannon says. "It's a beautiful morning, though there's a chance of rain later today, so I hope you thought to pack an umbrella or raincoat."

My coat is in my backpack, sitting next to my front door. I've been wet before. I'll manage. At least the air is warm, so I won't freeze.

"Trey is going to pass out your shirts. Please wear them for the entire competition. If you get cold, wear it over your jacket. That way, our camera people can easily spot you around town. There's a table over there to collect your keys, wallets, and phones.

Put them in the zippered bag with your name on them after you get your shirt. They will then hand you a phone and charger, which is everything you should need for the competition. Does anyone have any last-minute questions?"

One hand goes up. "Yeah. Can we choose our T-shirt color?"

All eyes swing to the table behind Trey and Shannon. There are some neon colors along with less retina-burning rainbow colors.

"Sorry, no. The shirt sizes were determined from your application forms. They're not one size fits all. Any other questions?"

No more hands go up.

"Okay, then, when I call your name, come up and get your shirts. Abbie and Carlos."

I guess we're going alphabetically by first name. I like being first because it should give us more time to check out our phone and see how it's set up. I toss my apple core and coffee cup in a nearby trash can and follow Abbie to the front. Trey picks up two blue shirts. I take mine and put it on over the shirt I'm already wearing. It fits more snug than I'd like and I already know this isn't going to work. I pull both shirts off, and put on the blue Amazing Asheville one. Now what to do with the shirt I wore over here?

"Give it to me," Abbie says, opening her backpack.

"Are you sure? I can wrap it around my neck like a scarf or something."

She shakes her head. "It's no problem."

"Okay, thanks."

Her shirt fits just fine over the tank top she has on. It looks good with her black shorts. My eyes continue down her legs and a laugh sneaks out of me. She's wearing knee-high compression socks that are bright turquoise with tacos on them.

"What?" Her glare sobers me.

"I love your socks."

She rolls her eyes.

"No, I do. You always had such fun socks in high school. Your fashion style is one of the things I like about you."

She doesn't believe me. "You're not funny."

"I'm serious, Abbie. Those tacos make me smile."

"They're tacosauruses."

"What?"

"They're dinosaurs that look like tacos."

I bend down for a better look. She's right. "That's even better. Where did you find them?"

"There's a store on Haywood that sells funky socks. That's where I usually find them. We should turn in our personal items so we can check out our new phone."

"Yeah, I was thinking the same thing."

Our race phone is an upgraded model of my current one, so it's easy to navigate. We take turns making sure the security measures recognize us so that no one else can open the phone in case something happens. While I still have the phone, I turn on the camera and put it in selfie mode. I lean in near Abbie. "Smile."

I snap a photo and see that she's looking at me rather than the camera and it's clear she thinks I'm nuts. "Perfect." I quickly make the photo our wallpaper and lock screen. "Now it'll be easy to tell our phone apart from the others in case they somehow get mixed up."

She rolls her eyes but says nothing. If she's already exasperated with me, her eyes will be worn out by the end of the weekend from so much movement.

When everyone has their shirts and phones, Shannon gathers us back together. "Okay, group. I want you all to have fun. When I say 'go,' take a photo of your team and text it to your race liaison, who will send back your first clue."

I look over at Abbie, a smug look on my face. We're already ahead of the game. I open the text app and add the photo, ready to hit send.

"Aaaaaannnndddd…go!"

My thumb presses the button, and a few seconds later, a message pops up.

Asheville is home to many impressive wall murals around the city. For your next clue, think smaller and find art that's just for fairies.

Abbie looks up at me with a twinkle in her eye. "This is going to be easy. Follow me."

She takes off up Broadway Street and I slide the phone in my pocket before catching up to her and matching her pace. I know where we're going, but decide to let her lead as she's so eager to do. We turn left onto Woodfin Street and jog the block and a half to our destination. Along the brick building are two groupings of tiny doorways along with a couple of individual doors. It's been a while since I stopped to really look at them, but apparently today is not that day because Abbie is on a mission. She holds out her hand for me to give her the phone, but I shake my head. "Crouch down next to them."

I'm rewarded with another eye roll, but she obliges. After snapping the picture, Abbie looking like a giant in front of the fairy-sized doors, I send it off. The phone beeps with the next clue and she rips the phone from my fingers, taking off before I can even read it.

"Hey, Abbie, what does it say?"

"We're headed to the old Woolworth."

More art. My kind of scavenger hunt. We jog down Rankin Avenue, passing a team headed in the opposite direction. After turning right at Walnut Street and left onto Haywood, we reach Woolworth Walk and Abbie tugs on one of the doors. Locked. She tries the other without success and then walks down to the other set. All locked.

"That doesn't make sense."

"What's the clue?"

"The answer is Reece Skyland."

"What about him?"

She hands me the phone.

This artist's oil and acrylic landscapes and depictions of the city skyline can be found all over the area. His work has even been featured on a Biltmore Estate wine bottle. If you haven't watched him work his magic, you're missing out.

This clue is much trickier than the first one. "I'm impressed you knew the answer."

"I thought I did. His paintings are in here, but we can't get in and I can't see his art through the glass to take a photo."

"You missed one tiny thing. It talks about *watching* him work."

"So?"

"He has a studio in the River Arts District."

"He does? Why are we just standing here, then?"

I try to hold in my sigh. This is going to be a long day of trying my patience. "I'll find us a ride."

She reluctantly hands me the phone and I open the ride share app, type in our destination, and get a notification that it will arrive in less than two minutes.

I show it to Abbie."Wow, fast response. I can never get someone that fast up north."

"Well, we are downtown. Plus, the chamber probably made sure to have drivers available for the competition."

"I suppose that's true." I hadn't thought of that. I narrow my eyes at Abbie's smug grin, pretending to be annoyed when I'm actually amused. It's nice to know she hasn't lost the spunk and confidence I remember her having in high school.

Our ride arrives and we climb into the back. I'm still impressed at Abbie's knowledge of local artists and have to ask. "How did you know it was Reece Skyland?"

"My sister tried the Biltmore wine at her supper club and raved about it to me. Funnily enough, it was the label she liked the most. She bought an entire case of it and plans to serve it every Christmas until the stash runs out."

"That's funny."

We arrive at Depot Street and climb out of the car. Another team exits the front doors of the studio and waves at our driver.

"Do you have another client yet?" the guy asks.

He shakes his head.

"Great!"

The man types into his phone. The driver's phone pings, he nods, and the two pile in and the car leaves.

Abbie looks at me, and I think I see panic in her eyes. "Remember that we all have the clues in different orders. That could have been their first clue."

"Still. Let's find Reece, get a photo, and move on to clue number three."

Without waiting for my response, she opens the front door and disappears inside. I sigh. This is supposed to be fun, but Abbie is starting to stress me out.

9

Abbie

I SNAP A photo of Reece working on a large painting of what looks to be the Blue Ridge Mountains. I was so enraptured by the scene; I didn't notice Carlos sneak into the frame and give a thumbs up until after I'd pressed the button. Thankfully, our photos don't have to be tasteful to get us our next clue. The painting's blue sky fading to pink and orange over blue and purple mountains is kind of mesmerizing. Maybe after this is over, if I win the money, I'll splurge on one of his pieces.

Carlos appears at my side and I realize I haven't even sent the photo off to our liaison. Yet another screw up by me. I'm sure he thinks I'm an ignoramus for not realizing Reece has a studio. *Get it together, Abbie. You're better than this. At least I packed all the stuff Carlos was supposed to in my backpack.* The thought makes me feel a little better. I send the photo off. Still, I want to get rid of the guilt I feel over my mistake.

"Sorry about getting the clue wrong."

"No worries. That was a tough one. I'm sure we'll get something I don't know, eventually."

I don't want his pity. Time to get back into competition mode. "As soon as the clue comes through, we'll be off."

He shrugs. "I don't mind if we take our time. We have until eleven thirty to reach the rendezvous point. I think we should enjoy ourselves while we do this. How often does an opportunity like this come along?"

"I suppose. Though it seems like you do cool stuff all the time. Or at least you used to."

"What do you mean?"

"Didn't you win a puzzle and logic problem competition in high school?"

"I did."

"And if I recall, you also took on a personal challenge of riding every ride at Six Flags in one day."

Carlos grins. "Oh yeah. That was fun, though they wouldn't let me on some of the kiddie rides because of my height."

"Did you sign up for this because it's another competition?"

"That was definitely part of the appeal."

"Why else?"

The phone pings with an incoming message.

Try your own hand at the art scene. Head to Studio 34, choose one teammate to participate in a hot activity that really blows.

The clue seems a little scandalous. "Do they realize how that sounds?"

Carlos chuckles. "Probably not, but I know what the activity is."

"Please enlighten me."

"Studio 34 is home to artists who work with glass."

The answer is obvious now. "Glass blowing."

"You got it."

"So, who should do it?"

"I have some experience with it unless you'd like to give it a try."

"Nah. It'll probably be faster if you do it."

"Are you sure? It's just ten. We still have plenty of time."

"I'm sure. Where's Studio 34?"

"Just a few blocks down."

I'm curious about how he knows so much about the River Arts District.

"Do you come to RAD a lot?"

He looks at me funny. "I do."

"I didn't know you were into art." My brain itches like there's something I'm supposed to remember, but I ignore it.

"I'm an art teacher."

While processing this information, my eyes snag on his muscled biceps. Since when have teachers been this jacked? Though I guess I don't really know anything about his life. I wasn't interested in keeping up with him after the thing with Rachel. He's probably the only person in my graduating class I'm not friends with on social media. In fact, this might be the longest conversation we've ever had. I must admit, it's not exactly a chore to make small talk with him.

"Where do you teach?"

"W. B. Hines Elementary."

He teaches young children? Why does this pull my heartstrings? I'm not even really a kid person. Don't get me wrong, I love my nieces, but I've never imagined myself as a mom. However, the thought of a very in-shape man being gentle with small people seems to awaken latent feelings about parenthood.

"We're here," he says, interrupting my thoughts.

I look up at the old building covered in graffiti in front of us. It definitely looks like an artist's haven. When we step inside, there are two other teams at work. There's also a camera crew getting shots of the people working with glass. I'm really glad Carlos is doing this. I'd hate to have my failure recorded for posterity. Carlos walks over to a guy in a white T-shirt that has the same design as ours. He must be our contact. I'm surprised when the two guys do a short, choreographed hand gesture.

"Do you know him?"

Carlos turns to me with a big smile on his face. "Abbie, this is Doug. Doug, Abbie. We play basketball together."

Doug shakes my hand. "Well, we sometimes play *against* each other. And we work together occasionally as well."

"Oh, are you a teacher too?"

Doug gives Carlos a questioning look. "No, we—"

"Anyway, Doug," Carlos breaks in. "Are you the man we see about our challenge?"

"That's right. Who's going to be taking part in the activity?"

"I am."

Doug shakes his head. "Well, then I doubt I need to tell you what to do."

Carlos gives me a sideways glance. "Humor me."

"Okay, well, your task is to make a glass pendant, marble, or icicle. The pendant and marble will entail using colored glass in addition to clear. What's your pick?"

Carlos turns to me. "What do you think?"

I shrug. "Which one's easiest?"

"They're all about the same," Doug says.

"I don't care."

Carlos studies me for a moment before turning back to Doug.

"Let's go with the pendant, then."

"Sounds good. What colors would you like?"

"What's your favorite color, Abbie?"

"Green, why?"

"Let's do green and blue. That should look nice together."

Doug motions us over to a table. "You got it. Have a seat and I'll get what you need."

There's only one chair, so I walk over toward the other competitors to see what they're working on. One team appears to be making a marble, but it looks more like a tiny egg with its oblong shape. The woman working on it looks frustrated.

At the other occupied table, a man has about an inch-long clear spike. Guess he's going for the icicle. I circle back to the table Carlos is at and find him already at work.

"Did Doug already give you instructions on how to do it?"

Carlos looks up at me sheepishly. "Uh, yeah."

I glare at him. "Did you start without him? You know, if you mess up, you'll probably have to start over."

"Have some faith in me, Abbie."

Right now, I trust him about as far as I can throw him, and I doubt I can even pick him up with as muscled as he is. "Whatever."

Doug comes over with two colored glass rods. "Let me know when you're done so I can sign off on it."

Carlos glances up quickly before returning to the work in front of him. "Will do. Thanks, Doug."

I'm not sure what to do with myself, so I take a lap around the studio, looking at all the glass art on display. Some of it is pretty cool. There's a small, rainbow-colored vase that catches my eye. I read the tag. *Double Rainbow Designs $45.* Expensive vase, but I can't deny how nice it is.

"That's a beautiful vase, huh?"

I startle at the sound of Doug's voice next to me. "It is," I say. "The name of the studio sounds familiar."

"Oh, yeah?"

"Yeah. I feel like I've seen it elsewhere, but I don't remember there being glass art."

"Well, the artist works with a variety of mediums. They paint, create wire sculptures, and work with clay. They even do some photography."

"Wow. Quite the jack of all trades. Or jill of all trades, maybe."

"You should check out the studio's website."

I pull out our competition phone and do just that. The home page is filled with photos of art in a wide variety of mediums. I'm mesmerized by the wire sculptures. There's just something so intriguing about coppery mountains and trees. I click on a link specifically for them and my mouth drops open when I recognize a piece. I turn to Doug and point at my phone.

"I have this."

"You do?"

"Yeah. I saw it at a booth in Woolworth Walk and it just called to me."

Doug smiles and his eyes seem to twinkle. "That's pretty cool. So, how do you know Carlos?"

All of my excitement at the discovery vanishes, and my smile drops. "We went to high school together."

"And you're still friends? That's cool."

"Actually, we're not. We were paired up together by some bizarre twist of fate."

Doug's forehead creases. "It sounds like there's a story."

While I'm tempted to share the sordid details with Carlos's

friend, my conscience gets the better of me. It doesn't hurt that I need him to finish the competition. "Not really. It's common to lose touch with people you haven't seen in over a decade."

"I suppose."

"I guess I'd better check on Carlos."

I walk back to the table and am surprised to find a nearly finished pendant. The center of the pendant is a swirl of blue and green. My breath catches. "Carlos, that's beautiful!"

He doesn't lift his eyes from his work. "Thanks. I'm almost done. How are the other teams doing?"

The team making the icicle has already gone, but the woman with the egg-shaped marble is still at work. A new team walks in the door and Doug waves to them.

"One team is gone, a new one just arrived, and a third one is still at work."

"Aaaand…done!" Carlos sets down his tools and lifts his hands like someone's just called time in a competitive baking show.

"Seriously, Carlos, that is amazing. Have you done this before?"

He shrugs. "Maybe a time or two."

I wave Doug over, and he gives us a thumbs up. "You've completed the challenge. Congrats."

Carlos stands and looks at Doug. "Will you take a photo of us with the pendant?"

I sigh, but protesting will just delay us from finding out the next clue, so I hand the phone to Doug and tolerate Carlos's presence next to me, even lifting my lips in a fake smile. Doug hands the phone to Carlos, who chuckles at the screen before sending the photo. He puts the pendant in his pants pocket, making my anger flare. Why does he get to keep the beautiful glass? *He made it, Abbie. What, you thought he was going to give it to you? No chance. He's not the kind of guy to do something thoughtful like that.* My eyes narrow, because something seems off about my internal thoughts. Probably all that talk about him teaching kids makes it seem like he should have a sensitive soul inside, but I know the truth.

For a second, I'd let my guard down, and it felt like a fun Saturday activity with a friend. But neither of us are spending time together because we *want* to. The only reason I've been playing nice is because I'm desperate for the money. Right now I'm feeling good about our chances. The phone beeps with our next clue, and I snatch it out of Carlos's hands.

This architect completed four major structures in five years for the city of Asheville using a unique style. Find the structures and the office building where he designed them.

Ugh. I have no idea who this is talking about. Reluctantly, and feeling a little sheepish about my impulsive grab, I tilt the phone toward Carlos, hoping he knows the answer. He meets my eyes and shrugs.

"Looks like it's time to do some research."

10

Carlos

FIFTEEN MINUTES LATER, we're in a car headed to Asheville High School. I haven't been there before because I've had no need, but now I'm interested to see if it looks anything like Douglas Ellington's other buildings, of which I'm quite familiar. When we arrive, I ask the driver to wait as we just need a quick picture and then we can continue into the heart of downtown.

I exit the car, wait for Abbie, and then close the door behind her. Together, we face the front of the school. The round archway of the main entrance and the spire at the top of the tower reflect Ellington's other buildings, but other than that, it looks like a fairly typical building.

Beside me, Abbie holds up the phone to take a picture and I block the camera with my hand.

"Wait! One of us should be in it."

"Why?"

The glare she's giving me could peel paint off a car, but I'm undeterred. I've been imagining creating a collage of our adventure, but I know she'd think it was dumb, so I scramble for a reason she might agree to.

"Because we should have some fun while we're doing this. We're on a once-in-a-lifetime adventure."

"Fine." She crouches down in front of me and snaps a picture, then holds the screen up. "How's that?"

I wasn't ready and my face is mid-smile. Also, you can see right up my nose. However, it makes Abbie snicker, so I let it go. "Perfect."

She snorts in response, but starts for the car without me.

I spend one more second appreciating the building. When I turn, Abbie's already in the car, motioning me to hurry. I guess we're not going to spend too much time enjoying the experience. At least not if she's in charge, which she obviously wants to be. I'd forgotten about how focused and goal-oriented she is. Another thing I respect about her, but it can get in the way of enjoying life.

A memory pops into my mind of her glaring at me in the halls at school. Which she did a lot those last few weeks of school, but this memory is from freshman year because she still had braces, whose rubber bands sometimes matched with her crazy socks. I wonder if she did that on purpose.

The car horn beeps, shattering the moment, and I hurry over to the car. Abbie's leaning on the horn. I get in, shut the door, and give her a conciliatory smile. "Sorry about that."

"Appreciating the architecture, were you?"

I grin. "Actually, no. Just remembering when you used to glare at me in the halls freshman year."

Abbie huffs out a breath. "We talked about that. It's just my face."

"I know, but before we were friends, I thought you wanted to murder me daily and never knew why."

"You're not the only one. So many people wrote comments in my yearbooks about my mean look."

This casual reminiscing has almost made her more agreeable toward me. I decide to keep the vibe going with more memories from the past.

"The rubber bands on your braces sometimes matched your socks. Did you do that on purpose?"

A small smile plays on her lips. "Yeah."

"I liked when you got all different colors to match those rainbow socks of yours. They were my favorite ones of all your crazy socks."

Abbie turns a puzzled look my way. "You ranked my socks?"

That does sound a little weird. "Not exactly. They were just the most colorful and seemed to lift your mood every time you wore them."

Abbie's forehead scrunches together. "They were my favorite, too."

I school my face so that she can't tell how pleased I am to hear that. What else can I talk about to keep her talking about not-so-touchy subjects?

The car slows to a stop, and I look out the window. We've reached First Baptist Church, the second building on our list.

"Do you want me to stay?" the driver asks.

Abbie nods. "Yes, please. That would be great."

I thank the driver and get out of the car. I stop on the sidewalk and my gaze runs up the enormous building. There's the familiar green spire on top of the domed roof. I really want to go inside, but Abbie is probably ready to head to building number three.

"Let's check out the dome from inside."

My mouth drops open and I look at her.

"Don't look so surprised. This is a pretty cool piece of architecture. I haven't been to Rome or anywhere else with an enormous dome, so I might as well see this one. Besides, I hear we have plenty of time to complete the remaining tasks."

I close my mouth and follow her inside. I know better than to gloat. I'm quite familiar with her vindictive streak.

The church is outfitted with wooden pews and a second-floor balcony. There are impressive-looking organ pipes, lovely stained-glass windows, and a gorgeous ceiling medallion. I turn in a circle, taking everything in.

"I'm ready when you are."

Abbie's standing back by the door. I guess she's seen everything she needs to see. Well, it's more than I expected.

"Let me see the photo," I say when I reach her.

She tilts the screen toward me. I'm in the center of the frame, my head angled back and my mouth wide open in awe as I take in the dome.

"You sure know how to capture my good side." My comment is rewarded with a wicked smile. We head back outside and into the waiting car. "To City Hall," I say to our driver. Abbie looks confused, so I add, "It's the next closest building on our list."

"Is it? I'm still not completely familiar with the city."

"You seemed pretty sure of yourself when we were looking for the fairy houses."

"I have a good memory and Rachel took me on a 'Quirky Art of Asheville' tour."

"Who runs that tour?" I wouldn't mind seeing if there's anything I don't know about.

Abbie grins. "My sister."

"Ah." I don't want her thinking about my association with her sister too deeply, so I get us back on track. "City Hall is near Pack Square, where we started this morning."

When the driver drops us off, Abbie turns toward the building and stares up at it. "It doesn't look like much."

"It's more impressive from a distance." We walk up the hill to the park and I turn around. "How about now?"

"It's definitely unique. The top reminds me of the church."

"The rounded entryways remind me of the ones we saw at the school."

She nods thoughtfully. "True." She backs up a step and holds up the phone. I actually manage a natural-looking smile in this one. "Okay, lead the way to the S & W Cafeteria."

"Yes ma'am. It's a short walk from here."

We head down Patton Avenue. She walks ahead of me and I take it to mean she's found her bearings.

"Here we are," she announces.

"Was this also on your Quirky Asheville Art tour?"

"No. Rachel dragged me here with some friends for drinks one night. It's pretty neat inside."

I notice the brewery insignia in the window. "It's a bar now?"

"More like a food hall."

We cross the street so that Abbie can take a picture of me in front of the building.

"You sure you don't want me to take some of the pictures?" I ask. My trip album won't be as fun to look at if it's mostly pictures of me.

"Nah, I'm good. Let me re-read the clue to make sure we've got everything."

I remember we need to find his office, but decide to let Abbie do her thing. If I can keep things cordial, maybe there's a chance we could be friends again. I'd really like that.

She looks up at me. "I forgot about the office. Do you have any idea where that would be?"

I shake my head. "No clue."

"Alright, let's see if Mr. Google will do his thing?"

I smile. "Google's male?"

She lifts a shoulder. "Why not?"

"I guess it could be. Kind of like cars are generally given female names. Mine's Trudy."

Abbie gives me a genuine smile. "Mine's Susie."

"Nice."

Her smile falters and her eyes snap down to the phone. "Anyway, let me see if Google knows the answer."

She types away for a bit. "Okay, I've got it. Sort of. It says his first office was in a building on Wall Street, but then he moved to the Flatiron Building a year later. Which one do you think it is?"

"Why don't we take a picture of both to be safe? They're right next to each other."

We reach our destination in just a few minutes. I point out the structures, then take the phone and angle us so both buildings are in the frame behind us. I attach all five photos to a text and send it to our liaison.

"I've wondered why there's a giant iron sculpture right here," she says. "I had no idea it represented a building."

"You should take an Urban Trail tour. You'll learn many neat things about the city."

"Maybe. I am enjoying being here thus far. I miss being able to go to the beach every day, but the mountains are nice, too."

I perk up at the realization that Abbie's given me an opening to ask her about herself. "So, you're an athletic trainer over at UNCA?"

"Yes, for the men's basketball team."

"Where did you move from?"

"Charleston."

"The South Carolina coast is beautiful. The job had to be pretty enticing to move away from there."

Abbie nods. "It was, though my boss isn't as great as I'd hoped."

I frown. "I'm sorry to hear that."

She waves away my concern. "No big deal. Just a...personality conflict. I'm sure it'll get better once he realizes I know what I'm doing."

"I'm sure you're a fantastic AT."

"Why do you say that?"

"You've always been so focused and hardworking. Whatever you put your mind to, you achieve. I've always admired that about you."

Her mouth twitches at the corners. "Uh, thanks."

I decide to press my luck with another compliment. "I'm glad we were partnered up. You'll keep us on track and do whatever you can to make it to the finish."

I feel something hit the top of my head. I look up and a raindrop hits me in the eye.

"Ow!"

"What happened?"

"Rain got in my eye."

"You okay?"

"Yeah, I'm fine."

The drops fall faster. Abbie looks around and then dashes under the awning of a nearby building. I follow and am safely under cover when the sky opens up.

The phone pings in my hand. She leans closer but surprisingly doesn't reach for the phone. "Let's read the clue together," she says.

I try not to give away the fact that I know this is a peace offering from her. I step closer until our shoulders are only inches apart. I hand her the phone, my own gesture to firm up the peace treaty forming between us. She cradles the phone between us and we stare silently at the screen.

Get your acting hat on. One of you is going to join the city's traveling history and comedy tour as a guest performer. Head down to Vroom Tours for your next assignment. Whichever person performed the last physical task is in charge of filming the performance of their teammate. Remember, comedy is simply a funny way of being serious (Peter Ustinov).

Abbie groans and I do my best to keep my grin under wraps. I cannot wait to see what she has to do. It's going to be way outside of her comfort zone.

"This is going to be so awful."

I nudge her shoulder with mine. "Nah, it's just another opportunity for you to show how awesome you are."

"Come on, Carlos. I don't have a funny bone in my body."

"Well, then, I guess you'll get the opportunity to grow one. Though we might want to wait a bit and see if the rain lets up."

Abbie shakes her head. "Always be prepared, Carlos. Weren't you a Scout?"

"Nah."

"Luckily I was." She unzips her bag, extracts two small plastic rectangles, and hands me one. She packed emergency ponchos. I'm not surprised and most definitely grateful. "Put it on and let's get going. We have a competition to win."

"Why do you want to win so much, anyway? Is it just a pride thing?"

Abbie is quiet for a minute. "If I tell you, you have to be cool.

No follow-up questions or 'helpful advice.'"

I have to work to keep my expression neutral even though her finger quotes along with the eye roll were humorous. Now I have to know. I cross my heart with my finger. "I'll be cool."

"I need a new car. Susie died on me and I've been driving my brother-in-law's, but I don't feel right using it when he's in town, so I'm currently without reliable transportation. Plus, rent here is outrageous and has dwindled my savings. If I win, then I'll have enough money for both and I can stop worrying so much."

Wow. I've just learned a lot. I really want to ask if she's bothered by the situation because she feels bad inconveniencing her brother-in-law. However, with all I've seen today, I bet it's because she doesn't like having to rely on other people. I don't know why she's so determined to do things by herself. My family helped me with the down payment for my studio. One day I hope to repay them, but even if my art career doesn't work out the way I'd like, I know they're just happy to have been able to support my dreams. But I promised to be cool, so instead I nod. "Thanks."

"For what?"

"For sharing. You've got guts."

The half smile lets me know she's pleased by the compliment. Maybe that's how I can regain her friendship.

Our ponchos on, I motion for her to lead the way to our next destination. "Let's go win this race!"

11

Abbie

A BRIGHT PINK bus with a giant mustache under the windshield pulls out of the parking lot as we arrive. We head inside and find our contact in a white Amazing Asheville T-shirt.

"Hi, what do we need to do?"

The man smiles at us. "Which one of you is performing today?"

I raise my hand. "That would be me."

"Great." He turns to Carlos. "That means you'll be a passenger on the tour and use your race-issued phone to shoot a video of her performance."

Carlos grins. "Sweet."

He holds out his hand, and I pass him the phone.

"Can I get the charger too? I want to make sure this is good to go for whatever magic I'm going to witness today."

I groan, but am pleased that he's thinking ahead. I unzip my bag and hand it to him. He finds an outlet and settles down on a green velour couch. It seems like an odd furniture choice, but it actually fits in quite well with all the eclectic decor in this room. It's been outfitted to look like a retro lounge. It's funky and pretty cool.

A throat clears and my gaze returns to the guy who was apparently talking to me while I was gawking at the room. "Sorry about that. I was just admiring the decor."

He smiles. "It's okay. This room is a lot to take in. As I was saying, you'll be part of the next tour that leaves in about an hour because only one team can participate at a time. Keith will drive you over to your spot, give you your costume, and walk you through what you need to say and do. After your bit, he'll bring you back here to wait for the bus to return."

"Costume?"

"Yeah." The guy's eyes are twinkling and I don't like it.

"How long is this performance?"

"Only about five minutes. It'll be fun."

"Suuuuuure." I don't believe the fun part one bit. "Can I wear my poncho over the costume?"

The guy frowns. "We'd rather you not, but it looks like it's already letting up, so you'll probably be fine."

I look behind me through the open door and see that it's now barely a mist, and the sun is coming out. Well, at least I've got that.

"Do we just wait until the bus gets back?"

"Either that or you can head across the street and get something to eat."

My stomach growls, and I look at my watch. It's nearly one. I'm surprised I haven't felt hungry sooner, though we've been pretty busy.

"That sounds good, thanks."

"Here." He hands me a rubber ducky with a number on it.

"What's this for?"

"It's your partner's ticket for the bus."

I turn and head for Carlos, who is asleep on the couch. It must be pretty comfortable. He looks so relaxed and peaceful. I take the opportunity to study him openly. He looks so different from the kid I remember in high school. That kid was short and stick thin with acne on his face. The man before me still isn't tall, more like average, but he's certainly filled out and is undeniably attractive. I wonder what he's done that's given him his muscles. Playing basketball doesn't do that. Either he's a weight lifter or does something else along those lines. If I ask, he'll know I've been checking him out and I don't want to listen to him tease me about it. I nudge his shoulder with my hand and he jolts awake.

"What happened?"

I shake my head. "Nothing. You fell asleep."

"Oh, sorry."

"No biggie. Since we've got about an hour before the next tour, do you want to grab some lunch?"

He gives me a sleepy smile that twists something in my gut. "Yeah, that'd be great."

He stands up and takes a few steps toward the door. I stop him with my hand and look at him expectantly.

"What?" He follows my gaze back to where he was sitting. "Oh, sorry!" He retraces his steps and grabs the phone and charger. "We're definitely going to need that."

I resist the impulse to roll my eyes. Across the street, we order and then find a seat to wait for our food.

It's awkward silence for a few minutes until I decide to ease the tension between us. Only so my partner doesn't get fed up with my grumpiness and ditch me, of course. I know I haven't been very kind to him. He definitely deserves some chastisement for his past behavior, but if I let the past ruin this opportunity for me, I will be devastated. "Were the couches in there super comfortable?" I nod toward Vroom across the street.

"They weren't bad. I just haven't slept much in the past couple of weeks."

"Do you have insomnia?"

"No, I've been working late."

"I know teachers work way more than what they're paid for, but that sounds a little ridiculous."

Carlos shakes his head. "It's not for the school. It's for my personal business."

Carlos has two jobs? That seems so responsible, not at all like the kid I remember whose sole focus seemed to be fun and adventure. He was always joking around. In fact, I thought he'd probably end up doing comedy somewhere. An art teacher was never in the realm of possibilities. It's too mature and adult. Though, maybe that's what he's become. Anything could have happened since I last saw him. Maybe he's no longer the immature kid I knew back then. I make a quick bargain with myself. I'll pretend like we have a blank slate between us starting now and let whatever behavior he displays now form an updated opinion of him. I could possibly be friends with a more mature Carlos.

"What else do you do besides teach?"

"I'm an artist."

I'm surprised, though I probably shouldn't be. He's always been a creative person. He came up with the best costumes for Spirit Week. Maybe it's his hobby or outlet to help him burn off steam and let loose from his more mature weekday job. *Come on, Abbie, give him a chance.*

"What do you make?"

Our food shows up and we dig in. I wonder if he's going to

answer the question. After demolishing half of his sandwich, he takes a drink and clears his throat.

"All sorts of things. My favorite is sculptures."

"Would you like to do that instead of teaching?"

"That's the goal. Though I enjoy working with kids, so maybe I'd hold a workshop or something."

Accomplishing objectives is something I have plenty of experience with. "What are your steps toward reaching your goal?"

"I'm not really sure. Maybe get some more commissions. Summer's almost here and I can spend my vacation creating new pieces and building up inventory. Eventually, I hope to have enough steady business to quit my teaching job and focus full time on art."

I frown. "That doesn't sound like much of a plan. How will you know when you're financially able to quit?"

Carlos shrugs and, for some reason, this casualness about his supposed dream irks me.

"I thought you were serious about being an artist. Sounds like it's just another one of your hobbies."

Carlos leans forward, his face suddenly serious. "What do you mean, another one of my hobbies?"

"Oh, you know. In high school, you were always trying something new. Stand up comedy, photography, drama club, kayaking. You never really stuck with anything. It seemed like every week it was something new."

He scowls. "I'm sorry we can't all be like you, knowing exactly what you want to do by the age of twelve."

"Hey, it's not a bad thing I'm so driven and able to achieve success. I know how to go after what I want."

"And I don't?"

"I don't know. Do you?"

Carlos looks away and I feel triumphant for a second until I see him deflate in his chair. Did I just hit a sore spot? I should probably diffuse the situation, but I'm not sure what to say. We finish our food in silence. When the check comes, I pay using the prepaid card on our phone.

We walk back across to Vroom in silence, a wall now between us. Inside, Carlos holds out his hand to me. I hand over the phone and charger and he sits on the couch, his face stony.

My gut squeezes with regret. I'm forming an apology in my head when there's a tap on my shoulder. "Are you Abbie?"

"Yeah."

"Great, I'm Dan. Follow me to the car and I'll brief you on what you'll be doing."

"Okay, just a sec. Let me tell my teammate I'm leaving."

I walk over to the couch and hold out the rubber ducky. He hesitates before taking it. "What's this?"

"It's your ticket for the bus. I'm going with the guy to get set up. I think the bus will board in a few minutes. Don't forget to film me."

I think the prospect of seeing me humiliate myself will at least elicit a small smile, but, if anything, he looks more upset. "I won't."

I want to apologize for my comments at lunch, but Dan calls my name and I follow him outside instead.

12

Carlos

ABBIE LEAVES WITH a guy wearing a white Amazing Asheville shirt and I'm left alone in the lounge. I decide it's probably prudent to use the restroom now before the tour starts and join the line in the hallway. Someone announces the start of the bus loading. I see the people in front of me also have rubber ducks, so I'm not worried about missing the bus. Abbie would kill me if that happened. Not that I'm too happy with her myself right now. I hate how she just dismissed my artistic ambitions. Just because I don't have a fifty-point plan like she would, doesn't mean I'm not serious about my dream. Who cares what she thinks anyway? It's not like we're ever going to be friends or anything.

When I board the bus, the only seats available are in the very back. Eh, I doubt our liaison will care how close the video is as long as I get it.

The Master of Ceremonies hops on the bus and we're off on

a comedy tour of the city. I perk up a little, listening to the emcee's silly one-liners interspersed with facts about the town. When he likens City Hall to a voluptuous part of a woman's anatomy, I laugh out loud. No wonder the city didn't let Ellington construct the county courthouse next door as well. We'd have had a pair of them. I can only imagine all the nicknames Asheville would have received if that had happened. I much prefer Beer City.

The bus heads north from downtown to a more residential part of town. I settle back in my seat and feel my body relaxing with the motion of the bus, the continuous chatter of the emcee, and the sunlight streaming in through the window. I warm up quickly and feel myself drifting off. Maybe I'll just rest my eyes for a few minutes until we reach Abbie's location, wherever that is.

I shoot up from my seat when something cold and wet hits my face. I drag my hand down my face and look up into the cold, hard glare of Abbie Price. Oh crap. I'm in trouble.

"Guess you're not dead," she hisses, tossing a water bottle at me. If looks could kill, I'd already be six feet under. I bobble it but manage to grab hold of it before it hits the ground and spills the rest of the water all over the bus floor.

"I missed your performance."

"You sure did. Now I have to do it again."

"I'm sure your next performance will be spectacular now that you've had practice." My attempt at a joke falls flat on its face.

She shoots daggers at me. I'm sure this will all be funny in the future, but Abbie's obviously not remotely close to seeing any humor in the situation. I switch to grovel mode. "Abbie, I'm so sorry. I didn't mean to fall asleep. I've just been exhausted—"

She cuts me off, her voice raising in volume. "Yeah, yeah, because of 'work.'"

Her sarcasm is cutting, but I suppose I deserve it. No use

defending myself. I've royally screwed up. "How can I make it up to you?"

She shoves another rubber ducky in my hand. "By not falling asleep this next time."

Words cascade out of my mouth. "I won't, I promise. I'll sit up front and be the best videographer possible. When does the bus head out?"

"In two hours."

"What? I thought the tours were every hour."

"They are, but two other teams are ahead of us."

My eyes widen. No wonder she's mad. I've gotten us way off track. "I feel awful. It was an accident, but I hate that my blunder hurt you."

"Whatever." She turns around and stomps off the bus. I follow behind like a chastened puppy. She plops down in a chair and glares into space.

I find it almost funny that her evil stare still hasn't changed after all this time, but the comment would not be welcome right now, so I keep it to myself. I look around for something to use as an olive branch.

"Would you like a snack or some water? I can get you some from the counter."

Her eyes snap to mine, and I take a step back. I stand corrected. Her evil stare has gotten much scarier.

"I've got both in my bag."

"Oh, right. Um, do you want to get outside, maybe find a park to pass the time?"

"No."

"Okay. Maybe I'll go get some fresh air for a bit, then."

"No. I don't want you wandering off and missing our bus when it's time. Sit."

I'm about to respond that I can tell time, but realize it'd just be better if I did what she said. I sit down on a neighboring couch. I lean back and slouch a little but then immediately stand up and move over to a wooden chair that is much less comfortable. I can only imagine what would happen if I fell asleep again. Although, a two-hour nap might help me power through the rest of the day. Should I ask her if it's okay? No, she already thinks I'm a terrible teammate. Falling asleep certainly added evidence to her already poor opinion of me. So much for getting her to see me in a new light.

Two impossibly long hours later, I'm still awake. That chair was awful, but it did its job. I could only stand it for about twenty minutes. Then I paced the room for a while and even resorted to lunges and push-ups. I may have embarrassed Abbie a little, but she did an excellent job of ignoring me and pretending like we weren't together, so all's well that ends well, at least.

The guy from earlier approaches Abbie. "You ready to do this again?"

She stands and gives me a look that would melt steel. I paste on what I hope is a reassuring smile and give a thumbs up. She shakes her head and follows him out without a word. I gulp, suddenly nervous. I better not screw this up again.

I walk outside and stand by the bus doors to make sure I have my pick of seats. A few minutes later, the woman from earlier opens the doors and takes my duck.

"You liked it so much that you're back again?"

"Not exactly."

She grins at me. "Yeah, I know. We all heard her laying into you earlier."

"I deserved it. She really wants to win, and I let her down."

"Well, then you'll just have to go above and beyond to make sure that happens."

"I guess so. Which side of the bus should I sit on?"

She points to the left side. I hand over my duck and climb the steps. I choose the first seat on the left and sit up straight like there's a board in the back of my shirt. My leg shakes as I wait for everyone else to board and the tour to start. I cannot get distracted and I sure can't fall asleep again.

We get underway with a different emcee from last time, though the beginning jokes are the same. I drum my fingers on my leg to stay alert. We head out into the residential area and I learn about houses that are now bed and breakfasts, see a face carved from a tree trunk, and a hospital where celebrities have stayed while dealing with drug and alcohol issues.

The bus stops on the side of the road. I notice a fake flower across the road that looks quite out of place.

"And now, folks, we have a very special guest today. Give it up for Betty Bee!"

I wonder if this is it. I open the camera app, lift the phone, and keep my finger poised over the red button. The bus doors open and I have to do my best to keep a straight face when Abbie's head, antennae and all, come into view. Her eyes find mine and I swallow hard as I press record. She looks away and smiles, but being only two feet away from her, I can tell it's fake. The rest of her body comes into view and she's wearing a very unflattering bee costume.

"Hey everybody, great to beeeeee here!"

A few people groan. I smile encouragingly and stay quiet.

"I was buzzing around looking for some flowers and saw this

giant, moving pink one and thought I'd check it out. I'm just POLLEN your leg. I know this is a bus."

More groans.

"Hey Betty," says the emcee, "know any good jokes?"

"I sure do! What is small, black and yellow, and drops things? A FUMBLE bee."

I chuckle, meaning it as encouragement, because I can see how uncomfortable she is. She really is a good sport to do this twice. Not that she had a choice.

"What do you call a bee with messy hair? A FRIZZ-bee! Why did the bee go to the dermatologist? It had HIVES!"

That one makes a few other passengers laugh.

"Do you know which musical artist bees like?"

She looks around, and it occurs to me she's soliciting answers from the crowd.

"Uh, the BEE-tles?" I say.

"No."

No one else responds and there's an awkward silence, so I try again. "The BEE-stie Boys?"

She smiles. "Sorry, not it."

"How about Justin BEE-ber?"

"Nope."

"BEE-yoncé!" someone shouts from the back.

"The BEE Gees!" says another rider.

"All great guesses, but the answer is Sting."

There's a chorus of groans.

"Alright, Betty Bee," says the emcee. "We have to continue on our tour, but I wish you luck on your pollination quest."

"Wait!" Betty, I mean Abbie, shouts. "Doth my eyes deceive me? I think I see the perfect specimen right out that window!"

She points to the right, and everyone turns to look. A few

seconds later, she appears in front of the bus and darts across the street. She grabs the flower and dances with it for a few seconds. "What, haven't you seen a courtship before? I like to get to know my beautiful blossom before the pollination process." She takes a couple of turns with the flower before riding off on it like one of those kids' stick horses.

"Bye Betty," the emcee says as the bus starts moving again.

I stop the video and play it back to make sure I got something we can send in. Watching Abbie do something so obviously out of her comfort zone fills me with compassion for her. I'd really like to help her win the money. I determine to do whatever it takes to get us to the rendezvous point before the end of the night and hope that a fresh start tomorrow is all we need. We were doing pretty good together before my epic foul up.

Might as well send the video now and see if I can figure out the clue so we can get back on track when the bus arrives back at Vroom headquarters. I hope Abbie won't be mad that I'm moving forward without her. In this case, forgiveness is probably better than permission. I hit send and get the response a few seconds later. It doesn't take me long to figure out where we're going next.

13

Abbie

I'VE BEEN LEANING against the side of the building for about twenty minutes. There's been nothing to do since my encore performance but pray that Carlos actually got the video we need this time. I was prepared to shake him awake this time if necessary, but he's obviously a smart guy because he was right up front and ready to go when I climbed the bus stairs. Oddly enough, I'd felt more nervous this time. I guess knowing someone I knew was actually witnessing my humiliation was key.

I've had a snack, some water, and visited the restroom. Without a phone to distract me, I've had to be content with people watching. Another team from Amazing Asheville recently showed up. I overheard the two guys talking, and this was their last stop before they find out where we're staying for the night. It's ratcheted up my nerves because we still have four more clues to go and who knows how many of them are physical challenges.

My stomach is churning with the fear that we might not make

it to the finish in time. As if confirming my sinking feeling, the last of the sun disappears behind the mountains in the distance. I can't even fully appreciate the gorgeous pinks and oranges of the sunset because my fear is turning to anger and all I can see now is red. This is all Carlos's fault.

My thoughts appear to summon the focus of my wrath, because the cheery pink bus pulls into the parking lot and down the steps he comes. The smile that was on his lips drops immediately when he catches sight of my face. Can't say I blame him. I'm well aware of the power of my glare.

"Did you get the video?"

He holds the phone to me. "Yeah, and I sent it off and received our next clue."

Well, at least he did something right. I take the phone from him and read the clue.

Take a break with Asheville resident Elizabeth Blackwell, the first woman in the United States to receive a medical degree.

I look up at Carlos. "Did you Google where she lives? Or lived, as the case may be?"

"We're not going to her house. Come on, I'll take you to the spot."

I'm tempted to hop on the internet to find out where we're going myself, but we're losing time fast. He better not be wrong. "Fine. Let's go."

He jogs up the street and I follow, appreciating the fact that he seems to realize we're in a time crunch. When we reach Pack Square, he leads us left past the Science Museum and stops in front of a metal bench. At our feet is a plaque with Elizabeth's name and relevant details.

I hold up the phone to take a picture.

"Wait. Get one of me sitting on it. The clue said 'take a

break.'"

"We don't exactly have time for a break," I say, but take one of Carlos on the bench anyway in case sitting on the bench is actually a requirement for completing the challenge.

I send it off. Carlos's stomach growls and mine answers with its own grumble. It's much later than my normal dinner time.

Carlos looks hopeful. "Should we get something to eat?"

"We don't really have time. I have a granola bar if you want."

"I know a nearby spot with quick and delicious to-go food." He holds out his hand and I reluctantly hand him the phone when my stomach gurgles again. "Do you like chicken, steak, or pork?"

"They're all fine."

"Great." He types away on the phone for a bit. "We're all set. We can pick it up in five minutes, which is just about how long it'll take us to get there."

The phone pings. "It's our next clue," Carlos says, taking a step toward me and turning so we can read it together.

Time to dust off your musical skills. Find the fanciest fast food in the city and wow the crowd with your best rendition of Mary Had a Little Lamb.

Carlos looks up and grins. "Guess I didn't have to order food after all. Oh well. Let's pick it up and then snag a car."

He seems very confident about the next location. How does he know so much about the city? I follow him back down the street. "How long have you lived here?" The words are out of my mouth before I have time to think about what I'm saying. I'm supposed to be mad at him, not curious to learn more about him.

"I moved here after college, so about eight years."

"What prompted you to choose Asheville?" The stressful day must have loosened the tight hold I usually have on my mouth.

"My parents moved up here while I was in college. I wanted to live near them and Asheville has a vibrant art scene, so I figured, why not?" He stops on the sidewalk. "We're here. I'll just run inside and grab our food. You get us a car to take us to Biltmore Village."

He hands me the phone and dashes inside. I look up above the door. *Blue Goose Tacos*. I like tacos, but I'm very picky. I hope these are good. The app says we'll have a blue SUV arriving in two minutes.

Carlos still hasn't told me exactly where we're going and I'm a little surprised I'm not fighting him more about keeping me in the dark. I must be tired. My stomach growls. And hungry. I should have a clearer mind after I eat.

The car pulls up just as Carlos exits the store with two large brown bags.

"How many people did you order for?"

He grins. "Just the two of us. Trust me."

The problem is, I'm beginning to and I'm not sure if that's a smart idea. "Here's our ride."

"Perfect timing."

We climb into the back. I can smell the food from inside the car and my mouth waters.

"Hey, man," Carlos says to the driver. "Do you mind if we eat in the car? We're kind of in a hurry."

"Yeah, that's fine. Just try to keep it in the tray."

Carlos smiles. "We will. You want one?"

The guy eyes the bag in Carlos's hand in the rearview mirror. "What'd you get?"

"I've got chicken BLT, bulgogi, steak, and pork cheek."

"The bulgogi would be awesome."

"You got it, man." He passes a small brown box to our driver. "Would you mind driving us over first? We're kind of in a hurry."

"No problem."

Carlos passes a small brown box up to the front, then turns to me. "What would you like first—chicken, steak, or pork?"

My eyes bulge in disbelief. "You bought me three tacos?"

"Trust me. You're going to be thanking me."

I highly doubt it. "Chicken, I guess."

He hands me a box. I open the lid to find a fried chicken tender with lettuce, tomato, bacon, and pico. There's so much stuff it takes me a minute to find the tortilla underneath. I take a bite and groan with pleasure. It only increases my appetite and I down the rest of it quickly. I need another taco, stat. I find Carlos grinning at me.

"You liked it, huh?"

"I did. I'll take another one, please."

"Sure."

He hands me another box, which turns out to be steak and cheese with lettuce, tomato, and pico. It's just as good as the first taco. He puts the third box in my outstretched hand and, though a word doesn't leave his mouth, the smirk on his face says it all. The pork taco might be my favorite of the three. When I finish, I'm a little bummed there aren't any more to eat.

"Those were excellent, thanks."

"I told you."

"Which one's your favorite?"

"They're all delicious. You?"

I shake my head. I'd eat any of those again. Multiple times.

"We're here," says the driver. "Where do you want me to stop?"

"At McDonald's," Carlos says, pointing up the block.

I give him a skeptical look. "You need some fries to finish your meal?"

Carlos smiles. "That sounds awesome, but no. It's the site of our next challenge."

The car stops and we head inside the restaurant. Carlos heads to the left and I follow, stopping in my tracks when I see a baby grand piano over in the corner. It seems completely out of place, with enamel tables and pleather booths on either side of the large black instrument.

"Whoa, what's that doing in here?"

Carlos shrugs. "Look up."

My eyes fly to the ceiling and there are gorgeous copper tiles and multiple chandeliers hanging down. I shake my head. A woman in an Amazing Asheville shirt stands next to the piano. We head over to meet her, passing a fireplace that's in the center of the room. This place is crazy. She smiles as we approach.

"Hi, there. I'm Melinda and will let you know when you've successfully achieved this challenge's goal. Who will be participating?"

We exchange a glance. "You did the last one," Carlos says, "so I guess this is me."

"Excellent. Please have a seat at the piano." Melinda turns to me. "When he seems to have it down, you'll need to take a video of him playing the song."

I sit down at a nearby table. I'm not sure whether I'm relieved it's not me or whether I'd prefer to have something to do.

The instructor places a sheet of music on the piano. "Have you played the piano before?"

Carlos shakes his head. "No."

"Okay, well, this is middle C, which corresponds to this note on the music. Place your right thumb there and your remaining fingers on the white keys. Your left thumb goes on the C key down here. Lovely. Do you want to start with the left hand or the right?"

"Uh, right, I guess because it looks harder."

I perk up at his words. He likes to do the tough things first? I kind of admire that. While he plucks out notes, I go through my pack to check the inventory. Our water bottles feel light, so I refill them at the beverage station. I think we've got enough snacks for whatever tomorrow may bring.

I'm hopeful that we're going to get through today despite the rough bit in the middle. Only two more clues after this, one of which is our rendezvous point. We've still got plenty of time, depending on how much longer this takes. I look over at the piano. Carlos's face is a mask of concentration. *Hurry up*, I silently implore him. Not that I think I would have been any better at this task.

Finally, after what feels like forever, Melinda waves me over.

"I think he's ready. Let's get it recorded."

I focus the camera on Carlos and nod as I push the record button. Partway through, I hear a note that doesn't sound quite right. Carlos emits a low, breathy growl and presses all of his fingers down, making a discordant sound. I end the recording and delete it.

"That's okay," Melinda says, kindly. "Try again."

I press record again. "Go."

This time, Carlos makes it all the way through and it sounds somewhat decent. The rhythm is a little off, but I can tell what it's supposed to be.

Melinda claps when he's finished. "Very good, Carlos. You've succeeded."

"Thanks." His smile doesn't reach his eyes. He looks pretty tired.

I press send on the text and am glad when we get a quick reply.

It's time for some fun and games. Head over to this geometrically shaped park known for its lively musical weekends. Find someone to play a friendly game of English draughts. To the victor, goes the next clue.

I think I might know this one. “Is this that tiny park downtown?”

“It is.”

“Great, but what are English draughts?”

Carlos shrugs. “Let’s find a ride and look it up on the way.”

14

Carlos

WHEN WE PULL up to Pritchard Park, the drum circle is in full-swing. The music is too loud for conversation, so I grab Abbie's hand to pull her toward the cement tables with inlaid boards for chess and checkers, but immediately let go when it feels like I've been shocked. I stare at my hand, wondering what that was about. Abbie has a perplexed look on her face and is staring at the hand I touched. Did she feel it too? She shakes her head, then wipes her palm on her shorts. I spot our contact, catch Abbie's gaze, and nod toward him. We walk over to a man and camera woman wearing matching Amazing Asheville shirts. Good luck getting much usable footage with as dark as it is. As if on cue, the woman points the camera lens at us and a light on top comes on, blinding me.

"You made it," the man says.

Abbie glances at the phone, and I know she's checking the time. "Let's get to it," she says, ignoring the camera woman and handing me the phone.

"Very well. Are you familiar with English draughts?"

"If it's the same as checkers, then yes."

The guy nods. "You have five tries to win the game. If you're unsuccessful, you will receive an additional challenge to complete."

"Whoa," Abbie says. "No pressure, right?" She chuckles nervously.

"Would you like to be red or black?"

"Red."

I should have known Abbie would choose the color that moves first. The man waves his hand over the table, which is already set up, and Abbie takes a seat in front of her pieces. I open the camera app. She looks so confident that I'm anticipating this challenge to be finished quickly. After a few minutes of play, Abbie's down to her last piece and her opponent has three kings. She forfeits the game and sets up the board again.

"You will be black this time," the man says. "We'll switch colors every round until you are victorious."

Abbie frowns, but switches colors. I hope she has better luck this time. I snap a photo of her face, deep in concentration as she considers her move. The combination of knitted eyebrows over focused eyes and slightly downturned lips shouldn't be sexy, but somehow it is. Probably because it reminds me of passing her in the hallways during our high school years. Her brown hair was always in a ponytail, swishing back and forth while she walked through the school like she meant business, mesmerizing me and every other guy in her path despite her no-nonsense expression. Yes, she was beautiful, but her self-confidence was what really made her glow.

Now that I think about it, I don't remember her dating much even though there were plenty of interested guys. Maybe she was worried it would distract her from her goals. I look her over, wondering how much she's changed. She's definitely still gorgeous and just as determined and self-assured as ever. There's no way I'm asking her straight out if she's dating because there's no telling how she'd take it. Better to just keep my thoughts to myself.

While I'm waiting for Abbie to conquer our current challenge, I decide to take a few more photos of her. I zoom in on a hand that's touching one of the pieces, then stand back a little to get both of the players in a shot. Then I focus on Abbie's face, taking partial portraits, focusing on different facial features. I notice little purple bruises under her eyes when I capture her brilliant blue-green irises. I put the camera down and study her face. Her rounded shoulders and droopy eyelids make her look how I feel—exhausted. This has been a long and busy day.

Abbie leans back against the hard, concrete chair and groans. She's lost again. After a third intense but ultimately unsuccessful battle, Abbie looks on the verge of a breakdown.

"Is it okay for me to offer some advice?" I ask the man.

"You can't tell her moves while she's playing, but you can say whatever you want between games."

"Thanks." I look at Abbie. "I used to play checkers with my grandmother all the time. Can I give you some suggestions?"

Abbie sighs. "I can't do any worse than I am right now. Go ahead."

I lift her out of her seat and draw her away from the table so the guy won't overhear us, doing my best to ignore the tingling sensation where my skin touches hers. The camera woman follows us over and I turn my face away from the light. I cup my hand around Abbie's ear and speak softly to make sure her opponent can't get any hints as to our strategy. When I pull back to look at her, she's frowning.

"That doesn't seem right."

"Since you're black, that's what you should do. I think it'll work. We'll do something different if you have to play as red."

"I'll give it a go. What time is it?"

"Don't worry about the time. Just focus on this game. That's all that matters right now."

She scowls, not seeming to like that I didn't answer her question, but doesn't argue. She returns to the table and the camera person follows her. I hope this works.

Abbie's competitor moves his first piece. She responds, and the match continues. My stomach is in knots, as all I can do is watch things play out. Despite her exhaustion, Abbie remembers my instructions and I think she just may do it. I pull out the camera in anticipation. Red sneaks by Abbie's defenses and gets a king. My heart sinks as her confidence evaporates before my eyes.

"It's okay, Abbie. You can still do it." Though, while I might know how to get out of this pickle, I doubt she does. A few minutes later, the game is over.

"I'm so sorry," she says. "I'm just tired."

"Hey, it's okay. You did really well that round. Let me give you some pointers for being red. I'm confident you'll get him this time."

"That makes one of us."

I give her a new strategy and an encouraging side-hug around the shoulders. "I believe in you, Abbie. If anyone can do this, it's you. Remember when you scored twelve points in the final three minutes of the basketball game against Robertson to get your team to overtime and then won by fifteen?"

Abbie's spine straightens. "Of course I remember that. How do *you* remember that?"

"I was there. A very impressive performance. One of many, in fact. You are the queen of comebacks. The ultimate Cinderella."

Her lips curve up slightly. "I don't know about that, but thanks for the pep talk."

"I'll be your cheerleader whenever you need it, but you've got this without a doubt. You're Abbie 'Ace' Price. You can do anything you put your mind to."

Her smile turns into a smirk. "Now I've got a visual of you in a short skirt with pompoms. That'll keep me up all night and not in a good way."

I grin, glad that I've been successful at buoying her spirits. "Maybe when we win this thing, I'll make your fantasy come true."

She shakes her head, but the smile doesn't falter. "Whatever." She rolls her neck back and forth a few times, probably sore from hunching over the board. My fingers itch to rub the soreness away.

"Okay, let's do this," she says, marching back to the table and sitting down with renewed confidence. She threads her fingers together and pushes them out in front of her in a stretch. She slides one of her pieces to the next square, then locks eyes with the man on the other side of the table. "Your move."

I perch myself on the table next to theirs and watch intently as Abbie makes quick work of a half a dozen of the black pieces. Soon she's got a king. Then two. A few minutes later, she hops over her opponent's last checker and raises it in the air in victory. I shout and throw both arms in the air. The phone in my hand reminds me I have a job to do and I snap a picture of Abbie and the man shaking hands, the black checker still clutched in her other hand.

I shoot off the text and then grab Abbie around the waist and lift her off the ground in a hug. "Great job! I knew you could do it!"

Her arms wrap around my neck and squeeze, but then go

limp. It triggers a warning in my brain and I remember we're being filmed. I quickly set her back down, let go, and take a step back, my entire body feeling electrified by our contact. My hand goes to the back of my neck. "Sorry about that. I got a little carried away."

Abbie's gaze is fixed on her shoes. "No problem."

The phone pings and our eyes meet. This is it. The last clue. I open the text and angle the phone so that can read it with me.

It's time to rest. Listed on the National Register of Historic Places, this destination has welcomed many famous guests, including F. Scott Fitzgerald, Helen Keller, Thomas Edison, Harry Houdini, Margaret Mitchell, Macaulay Culkin, Jennifer Lopez, and Barack Obama. It is also renowned for hosting the annual National Gingerbread House Competition.

Abbie groans. "Please tell me you know where this is."

I'm thrilled that I can answer affirmatively. I nod and type in our destination on the ride share app. "Our car will be here in three minutes."

"Is it far away?"

"About ten minutes."

"What time is it?"

"Almost eleven."

"Nothing like cutting it close."

I shrug. "We'll do better tomorrow once we've both had a good night's sleep."

"Sleep sounds amazing."

I couldn't agree more. Despite the late hour, the drum circle is still going strong when our car arrives. We get in the back and Abbie sighs. "This seat is so much more comfy than the checker bench."

She leans her head back and closes her eyes. I study her face, watching the light and shadow change as we pass under and then out of streetlights. I'd love to take a picture, but I don't want to disturb her. She looks so relaxed. I remember the photos I took earlier and look back through them. I text a few to myself. I can't help myself and text the video of Betty Bee as well. What Abbie doesn't know won't hurt her, right?

I feel something press against my arm and feel immediately guilty. Am I caught? I turn my head, an apology on my lips, but it dies when I realize Abbie's fallen asleep, her head resting on my shoulder. My chest fills with warmth and a smile slides across my face.

15

Abbie

A BRIGHT LIGHT startles me and I squeeze my eyes shut even more tightly. My head lifts and lowers a few times. What is up with my pillow? And why does it feel more like a rock than a soft, squishy cloud? My brain probably knows the answer, but it's not working at the moment. I lift my head and feel arms pushing me upright. Where am I? And, more importantly, who is with me?

The realization that I'm not alone is like a bucket of cold water and my eyes fly open. It takes me a minute to realize I'm not at home in bed, but sitting in the back seat of a strange car. Have I been kidnapped? I open my mouth to scream, but a familiar voice next to me causes it to stick in my throat.

"Hey, Abbie. We're here."

I turn my confused and tired gaze to the right. I blink in surprise when I recognize the face as belonging to Carlos. Did Carlos kidnap me? Is he trying to convince me to forgive him? No, that doesn't seem right. But what's going on?

"Are you okay? You seemed to be sleeping pretty deeply, but I thought you'd probably prefer to reach the checkpoint before we're disqualified from the race."

Everything comes flooding in. The race! For money I desperately need. Adrenaline rushes through my body and I'm out of the car in a flash.

"Let's go!"

He grabs my hand and pulls me up a set of stairs, through wide, heavy doors, and into the gorgeous two-story lobby of a hotel. My eyes yearn to stop and take it all in, but I ignore everything else, searching the room until I see the Amazing Asheville logo. All of my momentum recalibrates in that direction. There's a mat on the floor just like in the television show. I smile and jump onto it, Carlos's feet landing next to mine a half second later.

Trey smiles. "Abbie and Carlos, you made it with five minutes to spare. You're still in the competition!"

I sigh a breath of relief. "Thank you. Are we the last ones?"

He shakes his head. "There's still one more team that needs to check in. Here's your room key. Please be back here in the lobby at seven a.m. for a continental breakfast and your final instructions before you receive your first clue of the day."

"Um, did you say *key* as in singular?"

"Yes."

I turn to Carlos. Did he know we were going to be sharing a room? He doesn't look surprised. I guess that was something I missed at the orientation.

"I assume there are double beds in it," he says, still looking at me.

Trey nods. "That's what we requested."

Well, that's manageable at least. I hope Carlos doesn't snore. Though I'm so tired, I doubt I'll be awake much longer than the time it takes to brush my teeth and put on pajamas.

A thought slams into me. *What will Carlos sleep in?* He forgot his backpack, so I know he doesn't have a change of clothes. The thought of him sleeping in a bed next to mine in just his underwear sends a strange sensation shivering through my stomach.

Carlos takes the key from Trey. "Thanks. We'll see you bright and early."

He turns to me and gets a funny look on his face. "Are you okay, Abbie?"

"Huh?"

"You look a little flushed."

"Oh, no. I'm fine. Just tired. Let's find our room. I think we could both use some sleep."

We take the elevator up to our room. Carlos holds the door open and motions me in. I step inside, turn on the light, and freeze. Carlos bumps into the back of me.

"What are you doing, Ab—"

He must see what I see. A lone bed on the far wall. I step farther into the room, hoping against hope that it's an oddly shaped floor plan and there's another bed around the corner. There are a pair of club chairs and a desk with a phone, but nothing else. I look at Carlos. He closes his open mouth and swallows hard. This won't do at all. I stomp over to the table and yank the phone receiver out of its cradle. I hit zero for the operator. "Front desk," I say when someone answers.

"Front desk, Omni Grove Park Inn," a cheery voice says over the phone.

"Hi, this is one of the guests in room…" I hold out my hand and Carlos hands me the key. "Three thirty-seven. We were told we'd have a room with two beds, but this one does not."

"Oh, I'm sorry. Just a minute." I hear the clacking of keys for a minute. "I'm sorry, ma'am, but it looks like all of our double rooms are booked for the night. We could get you into one of those rooms tomorrow, if that would help."

"No, that would not help." My words are sharper than I intend. Carlos winces and I immediately feel bad for the receptionist. "I'm sorry for the rude tone. I'm tired. Thank you for your help."

I hang up and sink down in the desk chair.

"No more rooms at the Inn?" Carlos says.

I shake my head, unamused by his wit.

"At least they gave us a king bed. We can stick pillows in between us if that'd help."

I eye him warily. "What are you sleeping in?"

Carlos looks down at his shorts and T-shirt. "Uh, you have my other shirt, right? I'll just shower and then switch shirts."

I wrinkle my nose. He's trying, I can tell. It's not his fault we got this room. Well, actually it is, I realize, anger rising up out of my fatigue.

"If you hadn't fallen asleep on the bus, I bet we wouldn't be dealing with this issue. In fact, we'd probably have been asleep in our own *separate* beds an hour ago."

"Look, I feel terrible about that, but we're still in the competition. We'll start on a level playing field tomorrow and, after some good sleep, we'll be raring to go and beat the pants off of everyone else."

"Until you find some other way to screw it up." I mumble these words under my breath, but apparently not quietly enough.

Carlos's eyes narrow. "What did you say?"

"Don't worry about it."

"*What* is your problem?"

I shoot out of the chair and put my hands on my hips, affronted. Are we really going to get into this right now? Part of me knows it's not wise to let our tempers run hot when we're so worn out, but the hold on my tongue is tenuous. I have just enough to give a short plea.

"Come on, Carlos. Let's get some sleep. We can deal with it tomorrow."

Apparently, he's already passed the point of no return. His eyes look a little wild. "No. You obviously have a problem with me. Tell me, so I can apologize for whatever imaginary grievance you have against me and we can move on."

"Imaginary grievance? Imaginary grievance! My *problem* with you is not something I made up. You know exactly what you did."

Carlos gives an exasperated sigh. "Out with it, Price."

"You broke my sister's heart."

Carlos opens his mouth and then closes it again, his face scrunched in confusion. "I did what now?"

"She really liked Ryan Johnston, and you convinced him to not take her to prom. She missed the dance because she didn't have a date."

"I offered to take her, if you recall."

I scoff, waving away his words. "You ruined her chance at a magical night with Ryan."

"There is so much wrong with that statement. First of all, that was *twelve* years ago and second, it wouldn't have been a magical night, believe me. Third, I've apologized to Rachel, *the person I wronged*, and she forgave me. Why are you so mad about something that didn't even happen to you and no longer matters?"

His flippancy irritates me. "Just because it didn't personally happen to me, doesn't mean I'm not allowed to have feelings about it. Rachel is my *twin* sister, and she was devastated. Just because things seemed to have worked out long-term, doesn't mean what you did is okay. You weren't the one who had to listen to someone cry for several days. It shook her confidence in herself. She was reluctant to put herself back out there for a long time. Not that it turned out well the next time." I mumble the last sentence, not wanting to get into that right now. My beef is with Carlos, not Rachel's sleazy college boyfriend, Chris.

"Look, I didn't mean to hurt your sister. I was trying to do her a favor. Ryan was a jerk. She deserved someone better. I was just looking out for her," he says, his eyes darting away from my face.

My gaze narrows, things clicking into place. I see what's going on. "And you thought you were that someone better she deserved. Is that it?"

His eyes widen. "What? No."

"Yeah, that's what happened. You liked Rachel, but she didn't like you back, so you decided that if you couldn't have her, no one would."

Carlos shakes his head. "You're so wrong, it's not even funny."

"Your denial sounds weak to me. How did you convince Ryan to dump her, anyway?"

Carlos suddenly looks like a deer in headlights. He swallows, and his eyes dart around the room. I've definitely hit close to something.

"I'll tell you, but only if you promise to let me explain everything."

My stomach twists. I don't like the sound of that, but now I have to know. I nod.

"I need to hear the words."

"Fine, I promise to let you fully explain your treachery."

Carlos gestures to a chair. "Why don't you have a seat?"

"I prefer to stand."

He sighs, dragging a hand down his face. The regret that flits across his face surprises me, but I'm too keyed up to feel even an ounce of sympathy for him. "I had weight lifting with Ryan spring semester and heard him talking about asking Rachel to prom. He said they'd be voted king and queen for sure."

Ryan was always a little too cocky. Still not a big deal. "Okay…?"

"He said he would take her to prom and then sleep with her that night."

What a creep, but it still only sounds like typical teen boy bluster. "I doubt that would have happened."

"He seemed pretty adamant. I was concerned he might not take 'no' for an answer."

This gives me a brief pause. His concern for my sister should touch something in me, but I'm already on a roll and not willing to slow down. This confrontation has been a long time coming. "And you were worried he'd ruin the love of your life? Is that it? Rachel's a strong person. She can take care of herself."

Carlos pulls a face. "No, that's not it. I didn't like Rachel like that. She might have been fine if I didn't step in, but I'd have felt awful if something happened and I knew I could have prevented it."

Something about his words tells me there's something big he's leaving out. "So then, why did you?"

He squeezes his lips together and looks away. There's now no doubt in my mind he's holding out on me, but why? I try another angle.

"How did you convince him not to ask her?"

He looks away. "I, uh, told him she wasn't very good."

The full meaning of his words takes a minute to sink into my tired brain. "You what?!" The words explode out of me.

"I'm sorry, I know that was wrong, but I couldn't think of anything else that would deter Ryan."

"Is that why no one else asked her?"

"I don't know."

"Carlos! This is so much worse than just convincing someone not to ask Rachel to prom. You damaged her reputation."

"I know. I felt awful, but I was desperate."

"Because you were in love with her."

"No!"

"This doesn't add up. There's something you're not telling me."

Carlos scrubs a hand down his face. "You're tenacious," he mutters.

"So I've been told. Whatever it is can't be any worse than what you've already told me. Spit it out."

"I didn't tell you everything Ryan said."

I throw my hands up in the air, dropping onto the edge of the bed. "Oh my gosh, just tell me already."

"He said after he'd had your sister, he'd go for you next. He said you were the hottest girls in school and it'd be his crowning achievement to know which of you was a better lay."

My face scrunches up in disgust. "Gross! What a jerk."

"I know."

"And, what? You thought you'd be our knight in shining armor? You know he was just blowing smoke." I wrinkle my nose in disgust. "That would never happen."

"Maybe you're right, but I made sure it didn't."

My anger flares. "Yeah, by lying about my sister, tarnishing her reputation, and ruining prom."

"Look, I'm sorry for any hurt I caused your sister, but I don't regret it."

His lack of genuine remorse is infuriating. "Of course not. It didn't affect you in the least. You just continued on your merry way without a single thought to the destruction you caused."

His temper flares. "That's not true. It affected me just as much."

I snort with derision. "Yeah, sure."

Carlos opens his mouth but then snaps it shut, crossing his arms over his chest. "Believe what you want. Nothing I say will change your mind, anyway. It's late. We're tired. Let's get some sleep."

He's trying to deflect again, which means he's still holding something back. "I'm not done. This still doesn't make sense. We were friends, but not close enough for you to step in the way you did."

"Please let it go."

"Admit that you were into my sister, and I will."

He throws up his hands. "I wasn't into your sister. Will you just drop it already?"

"No! I need to know the truth. The whole truth. Why did you do it, Carlos? Huh? Why?"

"Because I was in love with you!"

The echo of his words lingers in the air between us. I've been shocked into silence. This is not at all what I was expecting. My brain tries to scroll through distant memories to find evidence for this confession, but I'm drawing a blank. I have no idea what to say to this. How is someone supposed to respond to a proclamation of former love?

Carlos looks wildly around the room like a caged tiger. He

shoves his hands through his hair so that it sticks up at odd angles. Is he going to lose it? "Look, maybe I should have just told her what I'd heard, but I acted impulsively. It's what teenage boys do."

All I can do is stare in disbelief. After a few awkward beats of silence, he turns toward the door. "I'm just gonna go."

Fear that I'm losing my competition partner finally kicks my brain and mouth in gear. "Where?"

"I don't know. To the lobby, I guess. See if by some miracle, they have a free room. If not, I'll sleep in one of the lobby chairs."

I don't like the thought of him trying to curl up in a chair. He's already exhausted. Another terrible night's sleep will not help our chances of winning tomorrow. I push everything I'm feeling into a corner of my mind and summon the rational part of my brain. "Don't do that. We can share the bed. It'll be fine. We both need to be well rested if we want to have any chance of winning tomorrow."

"Nah. I'm wired right now. I need to move. I'd just keep you awake."

He turns to go.

"Carlos, wait."

He pauses but doesn't turn around.

"Do you still have the phone and charger?"

His shoulders slump, but he removes them from his pocket and sets them on the table by the door. Without another glance my way, he leaves.

I fall back onto the bed, my mind spinning. Carlos liked me in high school? I had no idea. Why didn't he say anything? Probably because I didn't give him any encouragement. We hung out some because we both played basketball and traveled with our teams to games, but other than that and a few of the same classes, we didn't really spend time together. I shake my head. There's no way he was that into me. I would have known. He's probably just trying to get me to forgive him.

I'd like to call Rachel to talk to her about the situation, but the clock on the nightstand tells me it's nearly midnight. Too late to call. Besides, I realize, I don't have her number memorized, so I couldn't call her even if I wanted. Frustrated and more than a little overwhelmed with all of this new information, I try to distract myself by preparing for bed. I brush my teeth with the travel kit I stuck in my bag. I wash my face and change into shorts and a tank top for bed.

When I'm completely ready, with my clothes out for the next morning, I set an alarm on the phone and plug the charger into a wall outlet. I feel bad going to sleep not knowing where Carlos is, but he's a grown man who can take care of himself. A grown man who admitted he has feelings for me. *Had* feelings, I correct myself. He said he *was* in love with me. He's not *currently* in love with me. Big difference. A very important difference.

I lay there, staring at the ceiling. My mind keeps turning his words over and over in my mind. *I was in love with you. In love with you.* I know we're going to have to have another conversation about this, but hopefully we'll be able to get through the rest of the competition without a bunch of tension. A derisive laugh pushes out of me. Yeah, even I don't believe that for one second.

I toss and turn for hours, and the next thing I know, the phone alarm is going off. I groan. Today is going to be a *very* long day. I silence the alarm and look over at the other side of the bed, which is obnoxiously empty. Better go find my partner and see what kind of day I have in store. I drag myself out of bed and into the bathroom for a quick shower.

16

Carlos

I TAKE ANOTHER fortifying swig of coffee, hoping the caffeine will zip through my veins and fill me with energy. I know I'm going to need it, both for getting through the rest of the competition and dealing with however Abbie's feeling today. Did telling my version of events help or hurt me in her eyes? And what about that accidental declaration? Now that she knows I used to like her, she might be even weirder than before. There's only one way to find out.

I scan the lobby, but I still don't see her. My gaze moves to the clock on the wall. Six forty-five. She's still got fifteen minutes, though I expect she'll be down before then. I see several teams in various colors of Amazing Asheville shirts huddled together, talking quietly and casting glances at the other teams. More than a few eyes pause when they notice me sitting alone.

At least I wasn't stuck in the lobby all night. The front desk attendant found me an empty room, one with two queen beds in it. It was reserved for some of our competition, but one team failed to show up at the check-in point on time.

As soon as my head hit the pillow, I was dead to the world despite the turmoil still swirling around in my head. I suppose two weeks of minimal sleep will make that happen. The wake up call I wisely requested startled me out of my sleep coma and it took a few minutes for my heart to return to normal.

A hot shower helped me feel more human despite having to put yesterday's clothes back on. At least the complimentary travel kit allowed me to have fresh-smelling armpits and breath. My socks were still damp from yesterday's rain and smelled so funky I just tossed them in the trash. I hope I don't get blisters from my shoes.

Shannon and Trey enter the lobby and make their way over to yesterday's check-in spot. I look around for Abbie again, but don't see her.

"Good morning," Shannon says, looking very rested and cheerful. "Hope everyone got some good sleep. We'll get started in about ten minutes. Grab some coffee and breakfast from the table over there." She waves to the far wall. Where there were only coffee and hot water carafes a few minutes ago, now there are also baskets of breakfast bars, pastries, and fresh fruit. My stomach growls and I head straight to the table. I stick an apple and a couple of bars in my pocket for later and then fill a plate with a couple of pastries and a banana.

I find a seat near the checkpoint so I can hear when it's time to assemble again. I continue to scan people entering the lobby and notice when Abbie arrives. My eyes follow her to the breakfast table. When she turns, her gaze finds mine. Her expression is neutral as she approaches and takes the chair next to mine. Neither of us says anything. I peel my banana and take a bite, keeping my eyes straight in front of me. I can see she's sneaking glances at me out of my periphery. My stomach is rolling, wondering what she's thinking. As long as I don't say anything, I can't screw up, right? Best to let her lead the conversation.

"Did you sleep down here last night?"

It sounds like she's concerned, but probably just because a tired Carlos makes for a bad race partner.

"No. I got a room."

"How? You don't have any money."

"One team didn't show up, so they had an extra room after all."

She turns to me, eyebrows sky high, her mouth forming an O. She says nothing, but I know she's processing the fact that we only have eight teams to beat today to win the prize money.

I look down at the floor, but my eye catches something bright yellow. My head turns and I'm staring at sunshine-colored socks with the words "Everything hurts and I'm dying" in black writing on the side. I snicker.

Abbie turns to me with a scowl on her face. "What?"

I point at her leg. "Is that true?"

She looks down, and her forehead smooths out. "Not really. I just thought they were funny."

"I should be the one wearing those today. I could probably sleep for a week."

Abbie looks down at my feet and frowns. "Speaking of socks, where are yours?"

"I threw them away."

"Why?"

"They were still wet from yesterday and stunk to high heaven."

"You're going to get blisters."

"I'll survive."

Abbie shakes her head and reaches into the backpack next to her feet. She tosses something into my lap. "Here. Can't have my teammate limping around all day."

I pick up the tight roll from my lap and unfurl it. I'm holding a rainbow. "Are these from high school?"

"There's no way socks I wore nearly every week would have lasted fifteen years. Those are one of many replacement pairs over the years."

"Are you sure you want me wearing them? I'm probably going to stretch them out."

She waves her hand. "Just keep them. I have another pair at home."

"Thanks." I make quick work of putting them on. My feet feel much better in my shoes now that they have some dry padding.

"Alright, teams," Trey says. "Gather round. It's time for final instructions before day two gets underway."

We get up from our seats and move over with the other teams. As I look around, it seems like we're not the only tired pair. For some reason, this gives me hope that we still have a chance at winning. As long as there aren't any major screw ups like yesterday. I'll find some toothpicks to hold my eyes open if necessary.

"Today, there are eleven clues you need to decipher to get to the end. Like yesterday, they're all in a different order for each team, so you can't follow anyone else. The last clue is the same for everyone. The first team to reach the final destination will be our winner. Each team has been assigned a camera team that will meet you at each challenge. They will be wearing the same color race shirts so you will know who to look for. Does everyone understand?" Trey pauses and looks around at the sea of nodding heads. "Excellent. You will receive your first clue in three…two…one…now!" He waves his arm up and down like he's starting a Nascar race and there are a series of dings as the clues hit each team's phone. Abbie pulls ours out of her backpack and opens the message.

This sunny construction was home to one of Asheville's most famous writers. His controversial work alienated friends—first for being featured in it, and later those who'd been left out.

Abbie smiles. "I bet that's Thomas Wolfe."

"How do you know?"

"Rachel. She's told me about many famous writers connected to Asheville."

"Do you know where his house is?"

"No, but it'll be easy to find out."

Abbie opens a browser window. She starts typing but lets out a surprised grunt.

"What is it?"

She turns the phone to me. A warning message shows the battery is at five percent power.

I look up at her. "Did you not charge it last night?"

Abbie stiffens and glares at me. "I plugged it into the wall before I went to sleep. The outlet must have been broken."

Whatever happened, it doesn't help to cast blame now. "Okay, sorry. Let's find somewhere to plug it in."

Once connected to a power source, the lightning bolt appears to let us know it's charging. Abbie slumps down against the wall. "Ugh. The universe is against me. We'll never win now."

"Things happen. I'm sure we'll bounce back. We're two resilient people."

Her eyes narrow, and she crosses her arms. "Easy for you to say. You don't need the money."

Whoa, where is this hostility coming from? "In all honesty, you don't know what I need."

She blinks, surprised by my response, but then her eyes narrow. "Maybe I don't, but I do know what I need. A dependable partner who is as focused on winning as I am."

I don't understand why she's turning on me, but I can't back down from the challenge in her words. "Hey, I want to win this thing just as much as you do, but I also like to have fun. It's possible to do both if you'll just loosen up a little."

Her eyes widen for a beat before she levels me with a fiery, intense gaze, her voice an eerie monotone. "Are you saying I'm rigid? Who had enough supplies for both teams when *someone* forgot to bring their agreed-upon items?" Her words sucker-punch me in the stomach. "Yeah, that's right. *Me.* What have *you* contributed to our team? Oh, that's right, you single-handedly set us back hours, which almost lost us the competition. Soooo helpful."

Her words find their mark. She's right. I did screw up, but I've also helped plenty. She's too worked up to listen to reason, so I swallow my retort. Firing back at her will only make things worse. It doesn't look like our conversation last night cleared the air at all. It's clear she's only tolerating my presence because she needs me to achieve her goal. Then it'll be 'Hasta la vista, Carlos. Don't let the door hit you on the way out.' I was only fooling myself by thinking we could be friends again. There's no doubt about how she sees me and I'm grateful for one small mercy. At least she doesn't know I still have feelings for her.

17

Abbie

DESPITE MY ANGER, I know my words to Carlos are unfair. He's been more of a help than I'm admitting. But he did screw up royally last night. Of course, I'm one to be talking since we're now forced to stay in the hotel lobby until our phone has sufficient power because I didn't make sure the outlet worked when I plugged in the phone. Guilt descends on my shoulders like a weighted blanket. I'm lashing out because I'm mad at myself for screwing up. I need to apologize.

A shoe squeaks and I look up to see Carlos's retreating back. In the blink of an eye, he's out the front door and I'm left alone with the nearly dead cell phone. My stomach drops. Did I just run off my teammate? Maybe he just needed to use the bathroom or something. Yeah, right. There are definitely no bathrooms in the parking lot. *Great job, Abs. You let your temper get the better of you. Why can't you just let go of the past? Your sister has.*

I sigh. My conscience is right. I can't keep holding grudges forever because it's obvious now that I'm the one most affected by them. Why should I stay so mad about something that happened so long ago and has no relevance to anyone's life today? Rachel's fine. I'm fine. Carlos has matured. He really was just trying to help, albeit in a rather unhelpful way. *He did it because he likes you.* Well, he used to. After my latest tongue lashing, any hope of us being friends is toast.

What am I going to do now? It seems pointless to continue charging this phone when I no longer have a partner. Might as well look up the location of the Thomas Wolfe house in case, by some miracle, Carlos returns. I hate that there's no way to contact him. Of course, he can't get very far without a phone or money. Unless he hitchhikes, which I could very well see. If he's still somewhere nearby, then maybe I can convince him to keep participating. I look down at the phone. Nine percent. I need at least twenty to feel okay about unplugging it.

I look up the location of our next destination. When a photo of the bright yellow house pulls up, my educated guess is confirmed. This is definitely where we're supposed to be. I check the distance in the ride share app. Less than ten minutes away. I silently plead for the phone to charge faster.

When it hits twenty percent, I toss the charger into my bag, stand up, and head for the doors Carlos exited through about fifteen minutes ago. *Please let him still be around.* I push open the right one just as the left swings open and I find myself face to face with Carlos.

"There you are," I breathe out, relief flooding my body. "Carlos, I'm so sorry. I didn't mean what I said. I was just mad at myself."

His face opens in surprise. "Oh, uh, okay."

"I'm so glad you didn't leave. I promise I'll be a better teammate."

"Why would I leave?"

"Because I hurt your feelings."

He shakes his head. "I'm a grown man. I can handle a few harsh words."

I feel flustered and a little embarrassed. Why do I think he cares what I might think of him? "Oh, well, I'm sorry regardless. I hope you'll keep doing this race with me."

"Of course. I always fulfill my commitments."

"You just needed some time to cool off, then?"

"No. I went looking for this."

He holds up a palm-sized black rectangle.

"What is it?"

"It's a power bank. Now we can charge the phone on our way to the house. Have you called a car yet?"

"Where did you get that?" Fear that he smuggled contraband into the competition, which will get us disqualified, makes my words come out harsher than intended.

"From another hotel guest." He must see the distress in my eyes. "Don't worry, I checked with Shannon first to make sure I wasn't breaking any rules."

His words stem the rising anxiety in my chest, but I'm still dubious about his method of procurement. "I know you don't have any money on you right now. They just gave it to you?"

"Not exactly. I bartered with them."

"What did you offer them in exchange?"

"A piece of art."

I don't understand. My face must telegraph my confusion because he elaborates.

"I told the woman I'd paint a landscape for her."

"Oh, smart."

He rubs the back of his neck and looks out the window. "Thanks."

I scramble around in my brain for something to say to keep the conversation going. We seem to be back to a tenuous friendship and I'll take it because it means we're still in the race. I fall back on our current topic.

"How is she going to get in touch with you?"

"I got her name and told her to email me to work out the details."

A bunch of emotions run through me at once—surprise, elation, gratitude, regret. I can't believe I thought so little of him. He's a better person than I am. In his shoes, I'd probably have stomped off and not come back. Without thinking, I throw my arms around his neck and squeeze. The sudden weight throws him off balance, and he leans back, his hands coming to my hips as a counterweight. Heat shoots through my body and I'm stunned by the intensity. Mortification at my impulsivity trickles into my brain and I release his neck, taking two steps back.

"Sorry about that. Thanks for being proactive. I'll get us a ride." I take the power bank from him, plug the phone into it, and open the app, hoping I can get myself under control before I have to meet his eye again. *What was that?* "It'll be here in two minutes."

I continue staring at the phone, afraid to face Carlos after my hug attack. The car pulls up and we get in. The silence stretches between us. I sneak a glance at Carlos. His forehead is crinkled, and he looks deep in thought. My gaze travels down his body to his hand resting on the seat between us. I have the urge to see what our hands would look like with our fingers laced together. There's movement in my periphery, and I look up into Carlos's eyes. My cheeks flame, caught. There's tension between us and I need to diffuse it immediately. Unfortunately, my brain is drawing a blank, so all I can think to do is look away out the window.

Fortunately, we only have to endure a few minutes of this frisson before we reach the Thomas Wolfe Memorial, the official name for his former residence. I wave Carlos to a spot in front of the house, snap a quick shot, and send it off. A few seconds later, we have our next clue. I angle the phone so Carlos can read it.

Open since 1986, this alliterative business in the heart of downtown is a chocolate lover's dream. Pick a teammate to try their hand at the many layers required for sweet success.

My eyes light up because I know exactly where we're headed. I grin at Carlos, who looks befuddled. "I've got this."

"Okay. I'll follow you."

My smile falters. "One sec." I know where we're going, but am not sure how to get there from here. I use the map on the phone to set our course for the short walk. "Okay, let's go."

18

Carlos

A FEW MINUTES later, we're standing in front of Little Shop of Sugar. Abbie looks over at me and grins. "Ready?"

"I guess. How'd you know this was the place?"

"Rachel loves this place. I'm surprised you didn't figure it out since Jayson's your best friend."

Realization shoots through me. "Duh. This is Julie's store. I must admit, I'm not really a chocolate fan."

"What?" Abbie looks horrified. "Don't let Julie or Rachel hear you say that."

I shrug. "I'm more of a sour and gummy candy fan."

"Weirdo," she says but then adds, "me too."

Is she flirting with me? Surely not. "Shall we go inside?"

Abbie waves at the first employee we meet. "Hey Emily. We're here for the race, obviously."

"I figured. Julie's currently busy with another group, but I can take you back and get you set up."

Emily motions us behind the counter and into the kitchen.

"So this is where the magic happens," Abbie says appreciatively.

I spot Julie next to a guy in a neon green Amazing Asheville shirt and wave, though she doesn't notice. It looks like Abbie's going to be making truffles. I'm glad she elected to tackle this challenge. Of course, it means I'm up for whatever our next one is, but I'm not worried. I follow the women over to a table with a tray of chocolate balls. There are small bowls of sprinkles, chocolate curlicues in several shades of brown, and a couple of powders. A vat of melted chocolate stands nearby.

"Okay," Emily says. "First, everyone needs to wash their hands and put on these gloves and hair nets. Then I'll tell you what the objective is."

"Me too?" I ask.

"Everyone," she says firmly. "Even your camera person." It's then I notice the woman wearing a shirt the same color as ours standing to the side. "This is a kitchen and we're making product for the public. We take health and safety protocols very seriously."

When we're appropriately equipped, Emily continues her speech. "Today you'll be making twenty truffles. That paper there is the order and you are to make sure each one is constructed with all the proper ingredients. Right here is the list of each truffle's components. When you're finished, signal to me and I will inspect and give my verdict. Do you have any questions?"

Abbie grins. "Yeah. Do I get to take them with me when I'm finished?"

"Sorry, no. But if you do a good enough job, maybe we'll offer you a job."

"You're talking to the wrong Price sister. This would be more up Rachel's alley."

Emily chuckles. "You're right about that. She would save a ton on her chocolate bill with the employee discount."

"Well, Julie already gives her a pretty good one, so she's probably set."

"True. I'll leave you to it. Let me know if you have any issues."

I interject. "Is there anything I need to be doing?"

"Nope. Just take a photo of her with the finished product once it's been approved."

"That I can do."

Emily heads back to the front of the store. Abbie looks at the order sheet, picks up a chocolate ball between her fingers, and studies the truffle chart.

I'm twitching with a need to do something. "Do you want me to call out truffle ingredients for you?"

Abbie shakes her head. "No, just let me concentrate."

I sigh. The camera woman steps next to me, the camera pointed at Abbie. "Are you supposed to film us the whole time?"

"No. Just get some film of the various challenges and anything else I think might be interesting." She hits a button and takes the camera away from her eye. She glances at me briefly, before turning back to the action of Abbie making truffles.

"Cool. I'm Carlos, by the way."

"Yeah, I know."

"Oh. That makes sense. What's your name?"

She turns to look at me, smiling. "Savannah."

"Do you work for the Chamber?"

"No. I'm an intern at WLOS news station, but hope it will turn into a full-time job."

"That's cool. I hope it works out for you."

She nods her agreement, then lifts the camera back up to her eye, which effectively ends our conversation. I look over at the table and am shocked to see that Abbie's already finished four truffles.

"Abbie, you're a machine!" It comes out louder than I intended, and I feel several pairs of eyes on me. Abbie nods, but doesn't lift her eyes from her task. At this rate, we're going to be out of here in no time.

19

Abbie

I SPRINKLE SOME cinnamon on top of the last truffle before raising my arms and stepping away from the table. I've got to stop watching those baking competition shows. Though, I have to admit; it felt sort of thrilling pretending I was a contestant. Which, I remind myself, I *am*, which is why the adrenaline is pumping through my veins. Carlos waves Julie over to inspect.

She checks my creations against the order list. She looks at us with a smile and a thumbs up. "Great job, Abbie. You're good to go."

"Excellent," Carlos says, holding his palm up to me. I slap it, hoping this means maybe he's forgiven me for this morning. He holds up the camera, and I spread my arms out, palms up on either side of the tray and smile. Carlos lowers the phone and I drop out of my pose, shaking my head at how dumb that probably looked. I glance over at the other table to see the man is still hard at work. It gives me hope that we've got a chance to win despite our initial setback this morning.

The phone pings in Carlos's hand and I move around the table to see what it says.

On his twenty-first birthday, this wealthy bibliophile was gifted a chess set and gaming table that once belonged to a former French Emporer. See if you can find it among the treasures found in the Versailles of America.

Carlos opens the ride share app and types in our new destination. He then clicks over to the website and purchases two tickets for the next available house tour. I'm impressed by his quick thinking. It hadn't crossed my mind that we'd need entrance tickets.

"Have you been to—"

I slap a hand over Carlos's mouth and nod toward the other team, my other hand making the universal sign for quiet over my own lips. His eyes round and he nods. I can feel his soft lips pressed up against the palm of my hand and wonder what they might feel like against my own. The thought shocks me and I quickly remove my hand from his mouth, turning away and motioning for him to follow me outside. *Where did that thought come from, Abbie? You definitely do not need to be having any romantic kind of feelings for your teammate.* We pass by a team in bright pink shirts on our way out the door. Outside, I look around but don't see anyone. "Okay, now we can talk."

"Sorry about that. I wasn't thinking."

"No worries. To answer your question, no, I haven't been before. You?"

"Once or twice. It's pretty spectacular at Christmas. You should definitely try to go when it's decorated."

"Maybe I will. Does that mean you know where to find the chess set?"

He nods. "It's in the library on the main floor. If I remember correctly, it's an early stop on the tour. But, since it's self guided, we can get there pretty quickly."

A car glides up to us, and Carlos opens the door. "After you."

I climb in and he follows. "I wouldn't have thought to get tickets," I say.

He doesn't acknowledge my attempt at a compliment. "I'm impressed at how quickly and efficiently you made those truffles. The other guy only made five in the time it took you to make twenty."

I try to look unaffected, but his praise lights me up inside. "I have always thought I'd do well on those baking shows."

Carlos's face brightens. "Oh yeah? Which one?"

"I think *Sugar Rush* would be my jam because you get to make several types of treats, which means you have to be a well-rounded baker."

"The more competitive, the better, huh?"

"Yeah. What about you?"

"I think my skills would be best suited for *Nailed It!*"

A visual of Carlos beaming next to a cake that looks like an unsupervised group of kindergarteners made it pops into my mind and a laugh bursts out of me. "*Nailed It!* is ah-mazing! Oh, my gosh. That is the show I turn to when I need to unwind."

"Oh yeah? Me too. It's a spectacular disaster."

I smile at him, and he does the same. "It truly is. That's kind of funny that you watch baking shows when you say you don't like chocolate."

He lifts a shoulder. "It's just art with food. It's neat to see what comes out of people's imaginations."

I take a second to think about his words. "Yeah, I guess that's true. I never really thought about it that way. I'm more in it for the stress and adrenaline."

Carlos shakes his head, but his smile doesn't change. "That sounds about right."

He leans forward and addresses our driver. "What about you, Wendy? Do you watch baking competition shows?"

"Do you two know each other?" I whisper in his ear.

He shakes his head. How does he know our driver's name? He points to the laminated paper hanging down from the front seat that I'm just now noticing.

I nod, but there's a weird feeling in my gut. Wendy turns her head and her smile nearly blinds me. It makes her blue eyes sparkle even more. Her blonde hair is back in a ponytail and she reminds me of a young Reese Witherspoon. The feeling gets stronger and I know exactly what it is. Jealousy.

"No, I don't watch baking shows. I'm more of a physical challenge fan. Like *Ninja Warrior* or *Wipe Out*."

Carlos smiles. "Yeah, those are pretty cool, too. I've thought once or twice about trying out for *Ninja Warrior*."

She looks at him through the rearview mirror. "You totally should. You definitely look like you're in shape for it."

"Thanks. I just worry about all the obstacles that require finger grip strength. I'm not a rock climber."

She smiles wider. "I'm a member of the local rock climbing gym. If you're really serious about trying out for the show, you could come practice with me."

"Oh, yeah?"

"Yeah."

I narrow my eyes at her flirty smile. I am not liking what's happening right now.

"So, Wendy," I say, "have you been to the Biltmore before?"

"I have. You're in for a treat."

"Unfortunately, we won't have time for a full tour," Carlos says, "since we're in the middle of a competition, but don't you think Abbie should come back and visit the entire house?"

"Definitely."

The car turns, and there's a huge archway looming in front of us. "Whoa," is all I can say.

"This is just the entrance," Carlos says. "We have to wind our way through the grounds to get back to the house. It's pretty spectacular."

The car stops at a gatehouse inside the grounds. Carlos leans across me and sticks the phone out the window to show our tickets to the guard. He scans them and waves us through. My head is on a swivel as we drive down the one-way road, taking in the trees and flowers. We pass by a pond. Eventually, we reach a wall with an open gate and the car drives through. It stops just inside and the two of us climb out. Carlos asks Wendy to stay, and she says she'll park behind the conservatory.

The car drives away and we take a minute to appreciate the glory of the Biltmore house. It's huge and spectacular.

Carlos clears his throat. "I hate to interrupt your admiring, but our tour starts in five minutes and we still have to make it to the front door."

I almost forgot why we were here. "Right. Let's go."

We jog down the pathway that runs parallel to the front lawn and up to the line. Carlos shows our e-tickets to an employee who waves us up to the front. Another employee scans our tickets and points us to a display of brochures in multiple languages. I take one, but before I can open it, Carlos grabs my arm. We zoom past a sunken atrium filled with plants, through a room with pool tables, and into a giant two-story banquet hall. My mouth gapes open as I take in the organ pipes on one side, the table set for at least thirty people, and the enormous fireplaces.

Before my brain can fully process it, Carlos pulls me into another room with a table and fireplace. We enter a sparse, open space which gives me a backside view of the atrium, and then we're into a room with two pianos.

Carlos pulls me into an outdoor space and my feet root into place. I gasp at the view. Hills and trees stretch out for miles and the hazy blue mountains are visible in the distance.

"Nice view, huh?"

I turn to stare at Carlos. That's the understatement of the year. He winks, so I know he's being funny. "It's amazing."

"If you want to take it in, feel free. Our treasure is waiting in the next room."

His words remind me that this is more than just a day of playing tourist and I force my eyes not to return to the view for fear I won't want to leave. "This will still be here after today. My chance for twenty-five thousand dollars won't. Take me to the chess set."

Carlos nods, and we move through a long sitting area with three fireplaces. We pass through two huge wooden doors and I'm halted once again by the sights. This time it's the floor-to-ceiling and wall-to-wall bookshelves. My eyes travel up a winding staircase in the far corner to the second story of the library.

"I bet Rachel loves this room," I whisper in awe.

I turn back toward the room and look for a chess set. It doesn't take me long, as it's just to the right of where I'm standing. I turn to Carlos and stick out my hand. He shakes his head and motions for me to stand next to it. I comply, just barely containing an eye roll.

"I wonder which French Emperor this belonged to."

"Napoleon Bonaparte," Carlos says.

"Wow, that's really cool."

The phone pings.

Time to get more familiar with the reason a poll in The Examiner crowned Asheville "Beer City" four out of five times. Hope no one's afraid of heights. Go to the colorful, daring, death-defying brewery on the South Slope for your next challenge.

"Do you know which one this is talking about?"

Carlos shakes his head. "Search South Slope breweries. Maybe we can figure it out that way."

"Let's get out of the house first."

"Good idea."

He takes off at a fast walk and I rush to catch up. We pass through a large sitting room with tapestries on the wall and into a hallway. Carlos turns right and I see the front entryway. It doesn't look like the exit, but it's probably the quickest way out. We dart past the employees and into the sunlight. Carlos grabs my hand and steers me down some side stairs, through a rose garden, and around the side of a glass building to a parking lot where I spot Wendy's car.

On our drive through the rest of Biltmore's grounds, I search for breweries. A list with thumbnail pictures comes up and one catches my eye. The outside of the building is a swirl of color. I look over at the name and I know this is the one. I turn the phone around to show Carlos, and he grins.

"Yeah, that's probably it."

"Are you afraid of heights?"

He shakes his head. "No, but I highly doubt they'll make me walk on a wire. It sounds like a huge liability."

"I'm glad it's you doing it. I don't like the taste of beer, so we'd be in trouble if drinking it is part of the challenge."

I'm very interested in finding out what our next task is and glad that I get to take a break and watch Carlos tackle the task. I'm starting to feel grateful that we're paired up. His knowledge of Asheville has more than made up for my lack of it. I glance over at him. He grins and winks, sending a thrill through me. This both excites and terrifies me. *What is happening?*

20

Carlos

THE CAR DROPS us off in front of Flying Circus Brewery and Savannah is there to greet us in her matching blue shirt. There are a few other camera people hanging around outside. I know the presence of other camera people doesn't necessarily mean we're ahead of others, but it gives me encouragement that we're still in the running. I'm going to do whatever it takes to tackle this challenge as quickly as possible. I'd really like to win the money so Abbie can feel less stress. Of course, I could also use the money, but I'll be fine either way.

Inside, two competitors in Amazing Asheville shirts are already behind the bar. My eyes find the person in the white one and head straight toward her. "Hi, I'm Carlos. What do I need to do?"

"Hi Carlos, I'm Denise. Today you will take and fill drink orders. All beers are four dollars today. Your goal is to accumulate thirty dollars in tips from customers. Show it to me when you're finished and I'll confirm you are ready to move on."

"Okay. Is there anything else I need to know?"

She shakes her head. I pass the phone to Abbie and head behind the bar to the far corner, away from the other two competitors. There's a couple sitting on the end and I approach. "Hi, what can I get you?"

"I'd like a Jumping Lion. She'll take a Clapping Seal."

"Coming right up." I pour one of each from their taps, trying to remember the way to keep the amount of foam on top minimal. My only idea for how to pour beer properly is from viewing the commercials that come on during televised sporting events. Beer isn't my preferred beverage, so I don't have any experience using a tap. I must do okay because neither couple frowns when I set the glasses down in front of them. "That'll be eight dollars, please."

I'm handed a card. I call over to Denise and she meets me at the register to show me what to do. I take the receipt and card back across and set them down with a pen. The guy scribbles his signature and hands it back. I'm disappointed he didn't add a tip. This may be harder than I thought.

A woman approaches the bar a few seats down and I meet her from the other side, giving her my most winsome smile. "What can I do for you, miss?"

The woman giggles and swats my arm. "You flirt. Give me a Contortionist."

"Can do." I get a glass and it's a nearly perfect pour. "Here you go. That'll be four dollars."

She hands me a five and winks. "Keep the change." She reaches across the bar and squeezes my biceps before picking up her glass and heading over to a table near a window.

My first dollar. Only twenty-nine more to go. My best bet is to serve as many people as possible. A group of middle-aged guys are waiting to be served, and I walk down to them. I take their order and am rewarded with another two dollars. Six women about my age walk in and pick a table. Time to be proactive. I pop out from behind the bar and approach them.

"Hello there, beautiful ladies. I'd be more than happy to take your drink order and bring it to your table."

One woman raises a skeptical eye toward me. "I come here all the time and have never had the option of table service."

"You came on a special day. All beers are four dollars, and I will be your server for the rest of my shift." I wink to sell my pitch.

"Sounds good to me," says another woman. "I'll have a Lion, please."

"Great. What will the rest of you ladies have?"

I return behind the bar, repeating the order in my mind so that I don't mess it up. I find a round tray and place the glasses on it as I fill them up. I'm careful not to spill any beer when I pick up the tray and walk over to the table. I call out the names of the beer as I hand them out. "That'll be twenty-four dollars."

"Start a tab and I'll close it out when we're done. "

How am I supposed to get tips if they hang out for a few hours? My brain comes up with a response that may not necessarily be true, but won't hurt anyone. "It's pay as you go today because of the special," I say, hoping the confidence in my voice convinces them. "I can take a card to the register if you don't have cash."

"It's fine," one woman says. "I'll cover the first round." She pulls out two bills and hands them to me, a twenty and a ten. "You can keep the change if I can get a selfie with you. It's not every day I'm waited on by a hunk like you."

Crisis averted, I'm crouched down at her side within seconds. "Let's do it."

I smile widely, flexing to show off my physique. The woman studies the photo and then nods, apparently satisfied with how it turned out.

"If you ladies need anything else, just give me a holler. My name's Carlos."

"Will do," the selfie lady says, her eyes lingering on my torso.

Her blatant perusal feels a little uncomfortable, but I remind myself I'm in a competition and must use everything in my arsenal. I put the money in the register, remove the change, and pocket the six dollars. Nearly a quarter of the way there. I notice the people at the end have almost finished their drinks.

"You folks need another?"

"Nah, we're good, bud," the man says.

"Okay, well, have a great day."

He gets up and turns toward the door. The woman shoots me an apologetic look and surreptitiously slides two dollars under her glass before following him out. I pick up the empty glasses, stick them in the dish bin under the counter, and pocket the money.

There are now five of us competitors staffing the bar. If any more arrive, we're going to be fighting for customers. I glance at the table of women, but they're not even halfway through their drinks. Three women looking to be in their mid-twenties sit down at the end of the bar. I need to up my flirting game if we're going to be the first ones out of here. I roll up the sleeves of my T-shirt, flex my arms, and walk down to where the women are. I smile big, making eye contact with each one of them while I talk.

"Good afternoon. What can I get you fabulous ladies to drink?"

The brunette on the end leans forward on the bar, batting her eyelashes at me. "What do you recommend?"

I've got a bite. I bring my hand up to my chin, making sure

my biceps are flexed to their full glory. I drop into full flirt mode by deepening my voice. "Well, the Jumping Lion seems to be pretty popular, but I hear the Ringmaster's Delight is quite enjoyable."

A pleased look crosses the woman's face. "Oh, really? Then I'll try that one."

I turn a smoldering look onto the redhead in the middle. "And for you?"

Her cheeks flush under my gaze. "The same, please."

Two for two. Can I make it a perfect trifecta? I swing my gaze to the blonde woman on the end and am met with a glare that says, 'No way, Jose.' I straighten up. "What would you like?" My voice is all business now.

"Clapping Seal."

"Be right back."

When I'm far enough away, I exhale and chuckle. I guess my charm doesn't work on everyone. Speaking of people who are immune to me, I look around the room until I spot Abbie in the corner. She quickly looks away, but not fast enough for me to miss her eye roll. Does she not like how I'm working the crowd? I shrug and continue to the taps. She should be happy I'm using everything I've got to complete this challenge so we can move on.

I set the drinks down in front of the ladies, giving the first two another flirtatious wink. To the third one, I nod politely. "That's four dollars each, please."

I get exact change from the last woman, but make five dollars between the other two. I give them an appreciative nod. "Thank you, ladies. Let me know what you think of the Ringmaster's Delight. I'm Carlos, if you need anything else."

"*Any*thing?" the brunette says.

Her voice is heavy with suggestion and I fear my mouth has gotten me into trouble. "Um, another drink, I mean."

"What about a drink with you?"

"I'm, uh, not allowed to drink on the job, but thanks," I say, pretending I don't realize she's hinting at a date. I need an out. Now. I turn my gaze to the table of women and am relieved when one of them waves at me. "Duty calls. I'll come check on you again soon."

"Don't bother," says the blonde.

"It'll be my pleasure." I give the group one more big smile before heading out to the table. "Hello again. Does anyone need a refill?"

"I'm driving," one says, "but everyone else, please feel free."

I lock the order into my brain and head to the bar. I return, setting down five beers and one water. The driver smiles at me, obviously pleased at my thoughtfulness. "That's twenty dollars, please."

"I've got it." A woman in a Tourist's baseball hat holds up a card.

I take it and return with the receipt slip. She signs it and hands it back to me with a flirty smile. I see that she's given me an eight-dollar tip.

"Wow, thanks."

At the register, Denise hands me the cash and I stick the receipt on the nail with the other ones. Only eight more dollars to go. I serve a couple of people who approach the bar and am soon only five dollars from my goal.

Two of the women at the end are following me with their gaze, but their glasses still have about a third left in them. The super flirty one holds up her hand and motions me over with her index finger. I walk down to the end, a little wary of what might happen. I hope my smile looks more relaxed than I feel. "Do you ladies need something?"

"Yes," says the brunette. "My friend and I were having a debate about something and we need you to clear it up."

I don't like the sound of that, but it's not like they can do anything truly inappropriate in the middle of the day surrounded by people. "Sure. What's up?"

She points to the friend next to her. "Lexie thinks that since you have such amazing biceps, you must have a six or eight pack under that shirt as well, but Eleanor," she motions to the blonde on the end, "says your arms are the only thing you work because it's what everyone sees."

I know where this is going. It's certainly not the first time someone's asked me to show off my muscles. Maybe if I play along, I can get the rest of my tip money. "Is that so? And what do *you* think?"

She blushes. "I agree with Lexie."

"I appreciate the vote of confidence."

"So who's right?"

"Did you women bet on it?"

"No, this is just for bragging rights."

"Well, what do I get for revealing the answer?"

The brunette leans toward me and waggles her eyebrows suggestively. "What do you want?"

I grin and lean forward until our faces are a few inches apart. Her eyes widen and her breath hitches. Her gaze drops to my lips. "How about a five-dollar tip?" I say, my tone flirty.

Her mouth drops open, and she just stares at me. Lexie laughs. "I'll give you five dollars just for making Gina speechless."

She slaps a bill on the counter. I grab it and slide it into my pocket. "Thank you very much. And now, before I leave, I will answer the burning question."

I grab the hem of my shirt with both hands and slide it up a couple of inches to the waistband of my shorts. I pause and look up at the women to make sure they're paying attention. All six eyes are glued to my torso. A wave of satisfaction rolls through me at the attention. It's been a while since I've flirted like this. I've been so busy working on my art that I haven't thought much about dating. I'm enjoying this feeling of power. I tense my stomach before pulling my arms up to my chest for the full reveal.

"I knew it!" shouts Lexie and she high fives Gina.

Eleanor smirks, and I realize she played all of us. I shake my head and my eye notices Abbie marching toward me with a murderous look on her face. I drop my shirt and round the bar to meet her. "Hey. What's wrong?"

"Is this whole thing a game to you?" she says through clenched teeth.

"I mean, it *is* a game, right?"

"One I need to win very badly. Or have you forgotten?"

"I haven't forgotten."

"Then why are you flirting with women instead of trying to complete the challenge? You think everything is a big joke and nothing is worth taking seriously. I can't believe—"

I hold up a hand to stop Abbie's tirade. "I *have* been trying to complete the challenge." I pull the money out of my pocket. "Look, I now have thirty dollars."

The angry expression morphs into surprise. "You do?"

"Yeah. We just need to show Denise and take a picture."

She grabs my arm and pulls me over to the register. She yanks the money out of my hands and hands it over. "Here's Carlos's tips."

Denise counts the money and hands it back to me. "Great. Consider this challenge completed."

"Awesome." Abbie pulls the phone from her bag. I fan the

money out in front of me and smile. I hear the whoosh of the text being sent.

I hold out my hand to Denise. "Thanks for letting me do this. I had fun."

She shakes my hand. "You did great. If you ever need to make some extra cash, you're welcome to come serve customers. We're always looking for enthusiastic staff." She gives me a sly smile, and I know that she definitely witnessed my little strip tease.

"Er, yeah, thanks."

The phone pings, and Abbie practically drags me out to the sidewalk, shooting an annoyed look at Denise. Could she possibly be jealous of all the female attention I received during this challenge? The thought gives me a slice of pleasure and I decide to press my luck.

"What's with the manhandling? Are you trying to get me away from the ladies so you can have me all to yourself?"

My eyes meet hers before looking pointedly at her arm wrapped firmly around my biceps. For fun, I flex, which makes her blush. Her hand drops my arm like it touched a hot skillet and I chuckle.

"N-no," she stammers, her eyes now firmly on the sidewalk. "I didn't want anyone else getting any hints on where to go next, in case you blurted it out loud."

I smile. Her words don't fool me. She's definitely showing signs of attraction. However, I don't want to push her too hard, too fast, so I turn the conversation back onto the competition. "How many teams left while I was working?"

"None."

I let the satisfaction of that sink in for a second. "Well, it sounds like we didn't lose any time at least, but who knows which number challenge everyone's on."

"We're losing time right now talking when we should be figuring out the next clue."

"Oh, right. What's it say?"

"Former site of a tombstone business operated by Thomas Wolfe's father, this fifteen-story Neo-Gothic building is famous for being the first skyscraper in western North Carolina and features gargoyles on each corner."

I grin. "Easy. And it's walking distance. Let's go."

21

Abbie

I'M LOST IN my thoughts as we head up the street toward wherever our next location is. We're obviously looking for a tall building, but there are several, and at this point, I'm choosing to trust Carlos's intuition. He hasn't steered us wrong yet, unlike me.

I'm trying to figure out what happened back there in the brewery. Carlos's ridiculous flirting initially stirred something like irritation in my gut, but when those women started ogling his body, the irritation flared into something I couldn't contain. I'm glad he intercepted me before I reached the bar. I hadn't yet formed a plan for what I was going to do, but it probably would have ended with my humiliation. Or worse, disqualification from the race.

Why did women flirting with Carlos bother me? I shouldn't have any thoughts or concerns about his dating life. And yet, I can't deny the visceral reaction I had, almost like someone was intruding on my territory. Which is ridiculous because Carlos isn't mine and never will be. Sure, I don't hate him anymore, but that doesn't mean we'll ever really be friends. Even if that is something he was considering, I've been my worst possible self with him all weekend. We've both messed up during this challenge, but he's always kept an encouraging and upbeat attitude. I could probably stand to be more like him. I mean, he's friendly to all and funny. He spreads kindness wherever he goes and looks for the best in people. He's attractive and has rock hard abs, very firm biceps, toned calves, which, surprisingly, even look good in rainbow socks.

"Penny for your thoughts."

My head jerks over to Carlos, who's watching me. I'm so glad he can't read my mind. I can imagine how big his grin would be if he knew I'd just been thinking about his muscular body.

"Where are we headed?"

"The Jackson Building."

"Never heard of it."

"Jayson's law firm has two floors in the building. The floor plan is tiny because it was built on a twenty-seven by sixty-foot lot, but it's a cool structure."

"That doesn't sound all that small."

"It's enough for one small office and a conference room on each floor."

"I take it back. That sounds about like the size of my apartment."

Carlos smiles. "Mine too."

He turns the corner, and we walk a few blocks until Carlos stops and points up. "Do you see the gargoyles sticking out?"

I shield my eyes from the sun and can make out something jutting from the side of the building, but the glare prevents me from seeing any details.

"Smile." I look down and Carlos is crouched down in front of me, angling the phone up toward the sky. I scowl. "Well, it's not your best photo, but it'll do for the competition." He stands up and holds the phone out. The building towers above me and I can see right up my nose.

"So flattering." My voice is flat. Normally I don't care how I look, but I'm suddenly feeling a little self-conscious. Of course, I did the same thing to Carlos yesterday, so I have no room to protest. "How'd you get the phone, anyway?"

"I took it out of the pocket of the bag while you were looking at the building."

I'm a little annoyed but the phone dings and my focus turns to our next clue.

This landmark, established in 1938, has been completely restored and is the place to get an old-fashioned ice cream soda or milkshake, which can be enjoyed while also perusing products from local artists. Put on your apron and try your hand at the famous frappe.

It's about time I figured out another clue. "Now, this is definitely sending us to Woolworth's."

Carlos nods. "Lead the way."

I do a one-eighty, but my toe catches on an uneven section of sidewalk and my ankle twists as I pitch toward the ground. I tuck the phone into my body and turn so that my side hits the ground first. "Oof."

"Abbie!" Carlos is crouched by my side in seconds, helping me sit up. He runs his hand down my arm. I flinch and pull away. "Are you hurt?"

"Give me a sec." I close my eyes and scan my body. My shoulder and ankle are both throbbing. My arm feels like it lost a layer of skin. I open my eyes and lift my arm to confirm that there are small red scrapes. I hand the phone to Carlos before manipulating my shoulder with my fingers. The pressure only hurts in one spot, but nothing seems out of place, so I'll probably just end up with a bruise. I gently palpate my ankle and wince at the pain. I pull my other foot up next to it and the swelling in the injured ankle is immediately noticeable.

"Is it broken?"

I'd almost forgotten someone was with me. "No, just sprained. Help me get my backpack off. I have an ACE bandage, a first-aid kit, and some ibuprofen in there."

"Wow, you really are prepared."

Carlos takes the pack off of my back and roots around inside until he finds everything. He taps two pills into my cupped hand and passes me a water bottle. I take the medicine, then hold out my hand for the bandage. He shakes me off, opening the kit and handing me the wipes instead. "I'll do this while you take care of your arm."

I frown. "I'm an AT. I do this for a living."

"I know, but I'm pretty good at it, too. I've had my fair share of sprained ankles playing basketball."

That's probably true. Still, it's my job. He refuses to hand over the bandage and I decide it's not worth the fight. It's also taking up time we need if we want to win. I sigh, reminding myself that I can fix the bandage later, then remove a wipe and gently blot my skin, wincing when the cold medicine hits my scraped skin.

Carlos sits down in front of me. He unties my shoe and gently removes it, along with my sock, causing me to pause the work on my arm. I didn't know someone rolling a sock down my calf could be remotely sexy, but somehow it is. I try to cover the shiver that runs through me. Carlos looks up at me, concern crinkling his forehead.

"Did I hurt you?"

I shake my head, afraid my words would come out strangled if

I tried to speak. Carlos places the bandage at the ball of my foot, his hand holding it in place briefly as he wraps it around on itself a few times. The contact is so light it tickles and I grit my teeth to stop my foot from twitching. He makes a figure-eight pattern between my foot and ankle, keeping the bandage taut. He finishes wrapping and attaches the fastener. I'm impressed with how secure my ankle feels.

He rolls my sock up into itself until it's a band with just the toes visible. He looks at me to confirm that I'm in agreement before carefully rolling the sock back on my foot and up my leg. He loosens the laces on my shoe, cradling my ankle as he slides it on. I feel like Cinderella when the glass slipper is placed on her foot. That would make Carlos Prince Charming. I grudgingly admit the name suits him.

When my shoe is back on, Carlos grabs another wipe and cleans the rest of my arm. "Do you want me to put band-aids over the parts that are still bleeding?"

His question snaps me back to reality. "Oh. Uh, probably. It sounds like I'm going to be working with food."

He pulls out a handful of band-aids from the kit, chuckling when he sees they all have bright, colorful designs on them. "Perfectly Abbie," is all he says before covering my scrapes.

When he's finished, he returns everything to my bag, then stands and offers me his hands. Who knew he was so tender? This moment has me reevaluating everything I thought I knew about him.

I lift my injured foot and use my good leg to stand. I try placing weight on the wrapped ankle, but pain explodes out of the joint and a labored grunt forces its way out of my lungs. Carlos purses his lips.

He hands me the backpack, which I put on. He then turns his

back to me and crouches down, his arms out behind him like airplane wings. Dread washes over me. Is he suggesting what I think he is? His next words confirm it.

"Hop on."

"Carlos, no."

"This will be faster than you trying to hop on one leg. I'm strong enough to carry you, trust me."

Once again, my mind wonders why he's so muscular. I don't want us wasting any more time, so I place my hands on his shoulders and hop up onto his back. This is something teenagers do, not someone in their thirties. He wraps his arms around my legs and the contact of his hands on my hamstrings is startling, but the surprise is mixed with something else, something a little like pleasure. Our bodies are now touching from torso to hip, and this feels way too intimate. My mouth is near his ear and I feel a flash of mischief. I blow air softly onto his neck and feel him shudder beneath me. I smile, heady with the thought that this attraction I'm feeling might not be one sided.

"Uh, what was that?"

I freeze, embarrassed at being called out for my uncharacteristic behavior. Is there any plausible excuse for blowing on someone's neck? "Um, there was a bee, and I didn't want to risk it stinging you if I swatted it away."

He doesn't respond, which makes me wonder if he's buying my obvious lie. After a few seconds where I'm almost dying to know what's going on inside his head, he starts moving and reality returns. We're in the middle of a race. I can't lose my focus. Not when the end is practically in sight. I feel a hint of remorse for trying to distract him. He's doing a kind thing by offering to carry me and I'm not exactly helping him.

"You doing okay, Carlos?"

"I'm fine." His breathing sounds forced.

"Am I too heavy? I can probably hop or we can get a car if I get desperate."

"No, I'm good."

The question that hasn't stopped flashing through my mind pops out of my mouth. "How are you so muscular?"

He chuckles, but keeps moving. "I use a variety of materials with my art, some of which are heavy to move. I took up CrossFit to get me into shape so that I don't injure myself while working alone in my studio."

He said he makes sculptures. Perhaps they're made using concrete or stone. I could press further, but don't want him to exert himself more than he already is. Plus, if I continue to uncover more amazing things about Carlos, I'll have no choice but to fall for him, and that is something I'm afraid to do. What if he doesn't feel the same? It would be so awkward if we actually win this competition and have to work together on the tourism campaign.

The conversation lapses into silence until we reach our destination. At the doors, Carlos pulls one open and sets me down when we reach the counter of The Soda Fountain. Two other teams are already there, each with a competitor behind the counter.

A man approaches us. "Hi, there. Which one of you is doing the work?"

I raise my hand.

"Great. You'll make either an Old Fashioned Ice Cream Soda or a Milkshake, depending on who finishes first." He motions to the people behind the counter. "They both just got started, so you have a few minutes. Look around and I'll ring the bell over there when we're ready for you."

"Okay, thanks."

Carlos glances pointedly at my ankle. "Do you just want to sit at the counter and wait?"

"That's probably a good idea." I perch on a stool and look around the room. Something to the side catches my eye. "Is that what I think it is?"

Carlos turns in the direction I'm looking. "What?"

"Come with me."

I stand up, and Carlos offers his arm, which I ignore. I hop over to a booth and pick up a copper mountain sculpture. I turn and hold it out to Carlos. "I have one of these in my apartment."

He takes it and looks at me with wide eyes. "You do?"

"Yeah. Rachel brought me here once, and it just called to me." I gesture at the painting on the wall. "This stuff is gorgeous, don't you think?"

He passes the sculpture back to me. "It's pretty good."

"Pretty good?" I'm appalled at his lack of enthusiasm. "Carlos, this stuff is amazing. I never knew sculpture could hold so much emotion, but you can just feel the reverence the artist has for nature in their work."

The edge of Carlos's mouth quirks up and his eyes seem to sparkle. "I'm impressed you got all that from some twists of wire."

I shake my head. "You're supposed to be an artist. In this person's hands, it's so much more than wire. Isn't that obvious?"

He chuckles. "You sound like you have quite a connection with this guy's stuff."

"Why do you assume it's a guy? The artist could be a woman. The name makes me think that's probably the case."

"Double Rainbow Designs sounds feminine to you?"

I shrug. "I mean, girls are the ones who tend to gush about rainbows. They're the ones wearing rainbow-themed clothes most often." Carlos scoffs and gestures at his rainbow-clad legs. "Those are mine, a woman's. You're proving my point."

He gives a beleaguered sigh. "Fine, you win."

"Thank you. I learned yesterday that the artist works with glass as well. There was a beautiful rainbow vase at the place where you made the pendant. I may have to go back and get it if we win. It can be my victory memento."

When Carlos doesn't respond, I nudge him. "What's on your mind?"

"I like your idea of keeping something to remember this experience by."

"Indeed. What would you get to remember it?"

"I don't know. Maybe they'll let me keep the shirt."

I look down at my blue shirt, looking dingy from two days of wear, and wrinkle my nose. "I definitely like my souvenir idea better."

A bell rings and I set down the sculpture. I hand Carlos my backpack and hop back over to the counter. I'm handed a hair net and an apron, then directed to a sink to wash my hands. The man then points me toward an employee. "She will walk you through the steps for making the drink and I will be your taste-tester and judge."

I nod, ready to get down to business, then put on my game face, ready to make the best Ice Cream Soda this fountain's ever seen.

22

Carlos

I FOLLOW ABBIE over to the restaurant counter, but my mind is still turning over the past few minutes. She likes my art! Of course, she doesn't know it's my art. Should I tell her? Maybe later. Right now, I'm going to soak up her praise like a plant in a drought.

I'm concerned for Abbie's ankle, but she's soldiering on, so there's not much to do at the moment. I feel a presence next to me and turn to find our camera woman to my right. "Hey, Savannah. How has your day been?"

She smiles. "Pretty good. I've had some chocolate, got to see a handsome guy's washboard stomach, and now I'm talking to you."

Is she flirting with me? I'm not interested, but it won't hurt anyone to play along. "You saw a handsome guy today, huh? What a coincidence. I've seen more than my fair share of beautiful women."

I wink for emphasis and she giggles. She bats my arm playfully. "You big flirt."

"Guilty. How are you enjoying this filming gig?"

She shrugs. "I'm getting a good feel for the city, but there's not much to do between challenges. Luckily, you two made quick work of the last clue, so I haven't been waiting too long. I checked out some of the art in here."

"Oh yeah? See anything interesting?"

"Actually, I was drawn to the mountain sculptures at the booth you and Abbie visited."

Pride swells up inside me and comes out as a wide smile.

Savannah gives me a confused look. "You seem absurdly happy about that."

I really want to tell someone. "Can you keep a secret?"

Her eyes widen before crinkling in anticipation. She nods and I lean in so that my lips are right next to her ear. "That's my booth."

She turns toward me, amazed. "You're an artist?" I nod. "Wow, Carlos. Your stuff is fantastic."

"Thanks." My chest swells even further. Savannah holds her hand up and I high five it.

There's a loud clink, followed by a splashing sound. Savannah and I both turn toward the commotion. Abbie is glaring at us. An avalanche of ice cream and liquid from an overturned glass flow over the edge of the counter onto the floor. I feel immediate guilt that I wasn't paying attention.

Beside me, Savannah flinches. "Oops. I'm supposed to be filming her." She lifts the camera up to her eye.

I hustle to the counter and grab some napkins to clean up the mess. "I'll get this. You do whatever you need to do."

Abbie says nothing, but the evil eye she's giving me speaks

volumes. I'm suitably chastened and determine to stay focused on supporting my teammate however I can. "You can do it, Abbie. Take your time."

She huffs out a breath and then turns her back on me. Someone tosses me a rag, which works much better than the flimsy napkins I was using. I find a trash can to dump the soggy paper and wipe the counter once more to make sure it's not sticky. Action complete, I'm not sure what to do with myself, so I sit down at the counter to watch, surprised that she's almost finished with the new concoction.

Abbie adds a scoop of strawberry ice cream to the top of the full glass. My mouth waters. It looks amazing. She adds whipped cream, a cherry, and a straw. It looks picture perfect. I want that in my belly. She slides it down the counter next to a silver call bell and pushes the plunger down. The crisp ding brings over the man, who gave instructions. He eyes the frosty glass before picking it up and taking a sip. He nods, sets it back down, and gives a thumbs up. Abbie beams. I remember my job and hold up the phone, taking a photo of her standing behind her creation.

By the time Abbie removes her apron and hairnet, we have our next clue. I hold the phone out between us.

This cafe looks like it belongs across the pond. It'll make you want to say 'Cheerio. Fancy a cuppa?'

"That must be—"

Abbie slaps her hand across my mouth and I'm really tempted to kiss it. However, this is not the time nor the place. "Not here," she chides.

Can she read my thoughts? Surely not. Though I wish her response was to my thoughts. Then that would mean she's open to being kissed by me at a more prudent time and location. If only. I nod, and she takes her hand away. I bend my knees, offering her my back, but she ignores me and hops through the building and out to the sidewalk. Once outside, she looks at me with raised eyebrows, my signal to finish my sentence.

"I think we're supposed to go to DeeDee's Coffee. It's housed in a red double-decker bus."

"Let's go."

I hesitate. "It's about four blocks away. Are you sure I can't give you a ride?"

She pauses, then nods. "Fine."

I turn my back to her and she hops up, wrapping her arms over my shoulders and across my chest. This thrills me more than it probably should. I love having an excuse to be this close to her. I place my hands under her thighs, shift her up a little higher on my back, and take off toward the cafe.

"You and our camera person looked like you were having fun back there."

My toe hits a raised section of sidewalk and I stumble a bit but quickly recover. I'd feel terrible if I dropped Abbie. "We were just talking."

"Just talking? It looked like you were telling secrets."

Her words have an edge to them and I wonder what I've done this time to upset her. I try to diffuse the situation with a joke. "If I didn't already know how much you dislike me, I'd almost think you were a little jealous."

Instead of the sharp retort I'm expecting, there's a long beat of silence. Did I go too far? "Abbie?"

She snorts. "You wish."

"Maybe I do." I regret the words the instant they leave my mouth. I didn't mean to speak the truth. Hopefully, she'll think I'm still messing around. I change the subject. "When we win the money, what kind of car are you going to get to replace Susie?"

"Not sure yet. I want four-wheel drive for hiking, so maybe another Jeep."

"Where do you like to hike?"

"I haven't had much time to hike here yet, but I did a good amount back in Charleston."

I feel her slipping down my back so I stop walking long enough to hoist her higher on my body, then continue toward our destination. "There aren't any mountains on the coast. What kind of hiking did you do there?"

"Mainly nature hikes. You can see a variety of animals and get some magnificent water views. Most of the hiking requires a bit of a drive, but I've taken some gorgeous sunrise photos."

"Oh yeah? I'd love to see them."

"I've posted some on my website."

She has a website? "What's your website for?"

"I have a blog of my travels and adventures. I also talk some about my experiences as a female athletic trainer. Though I haven't been able to do any traveling since I moved up here."

"I'll have to check it out." Mentally, I make a note to send her a list of local places to explore.

"What about you?"

"What about me *what*?"

"I assume you have a website for your art."

"Oh. Yeah, I do."

"We can swap addresses when we get our phones back."

"Sure." I'm relieved she didn't ask me for it now. I'm not sure I'm ready to deal with whatever might happen when she finds out who I am. Though, perhaps it would soften her toward me a little more. Or make her mad about withholding pertinent information. It's hard to tell which way she'd go. She's been hard to read today.

I look up the block and see a glimmer of red. We're almost

there. Half a minute later, we're standing in front of the bus. I set Abbie down and take the phone out of my pocket. She grabs it from me and motions for me to back up closer to the cafe. I stick my hands in my pocket and smile.

She lowers the phone and I return to her side, interested in learning our next location. Only four left. We're so close. The phone pings with our new clue.

Batter up! This next challenge will be out of this world. Get ready to show off your souvenir distribution skills as this lunar mascot.

"Mr. Moon!" we shout simultaneously.

I catch Abbie's eye and we grin. "To McCormick field," she says.

23

Abbie

THE CAR DROPS us off at the front gates and we head inside to meet a guy in a Tourists' jersey open over an Amazing Asheville shirt. I'm almost tired of seeing that shirt, but I remind myself we're so close to the finish line. Imagining the peace of mind that would come with having a reliable car and a small nest egg of savings pushes the annoyance from my mind.

"Hey, I'm Zander, the current Mr. Moon. Today, one of you will don the costume and you'll be shooting the T-shirt cannon."

"Alright!" Carlos pumps his arm. "I've wanted to shoot one of those. They look so fun."

"There are three targets set up in the stands. Your job is to hit each one with a shirt from that spot on the field." He motions to a blue bullseye in the grass near the dugout.

Carlos rubs his hands together. "I like the sound of this

challenge."

I pout. "Yeah, this sounds much easier than making truffles."

Carlos grabs my shoulder and squeezes. "But you did great at that challenge. You smoked that other guy."

My down-turned lips curve up in response to his praise. Would he be this encouraging and complimentary to someone he was dating? Probably. He just seems like that kind of person. *Why am I even thinking about this?*

Carlos turns back to Zander. "Let's get cracking!"

"Great," says Zander, then turns to me. "You can take a seat in the stands and watch the fun."

A few camera people are spread out in seats. My eye catches on our camera woman who waves at me. The small smile disappears and I have to focus to keep my face neutral. I don't like how flirty she's been with Carlos. He was right. I *am* a little jealous, but I'll never tell him that.

She motions me over. It's just my luck that she's in the front row. If she was higher, I could use my ankle as an excuse. I shouldn't be unkind to her. It's not her fault I have these conflicting feelings rolling around inside. I hop over and sit next to her.

"Hey, uh..." I pause, realizing I don't know her name.

"Savannah," she says, holding out her hand.

I shake it. "Why aren't you sitting up with the other camera folks?"

"I didn't want you to have to hop up stairs with your hurt ankle."

Now I do feel like a jerk. She's so nice. And pretty. There's nothing wrong with two single people flirting with one another. "Thanks. That was very kind of you."

"After this, I won't see you two again until the finish line."

I turn to face her. "This is our last challenge?"

Her hand shoots up over her mouth. "Oops. I don't think I was supposed to tell you that. "

I'm excited about this information. That means we just have to find two more locations and then the finish. She looks distraught, and I pat her arm. "I'm sure it's fine. We still have to figure out where we're going. It actually makes sense. Yesterday we had four challenges, and this is our fourth one today."

She still looks crestfallen. I search for something else to say to reassure her, but I'm distracted by the appearance of Carlos. I mean, Mr. Moon. "There he is." I point.

Savannah picks up the camera from her lap and turns it on. Carlos comes over to where we are and poses, the T-shirt cannon slung over one shoulder. I laugh as he hams it up for the camera.

"I can hardly see anything." The costume helmet muffles his words.

He turns and heads over to his spot on the field. Zander shows him how to work the cannon and he tries it. The first shirt sails way over the first target. His second attempt is just above it and to the left, but the third finds its mark.

"Yes!" I clap. We might be out of here in no time.

The second target takes Carlos six tries. He hits the third in two. I leap up from my seat, cheering, and then wince when I put too much weight on my sore ankle. I hobble my way down to the field. Carlos removes the moon head. His face is slick with sweat.

"Ooh boy, it is hot in here."

I wrinkle my nose. "You smell, too. It reminds me of the men's locker room at UNCA."

He gives me a pointed look. "Thanks."

I shrug. "I just call it like I see it. Great job, by the way. You're a true marksman."

"Thanks. It's hard to see in this head."

"Put it back on."

"What? Abbie, I'm burning up."

"I have to take a picture."

"Just take it without the head. Then they know it's me."

"Fine." I snap his picture.

He wriggles out of the rest of the costume, and his shirt is plastered to his torso. It really must be hot in those costumes. I don't know how anyone does it for multiple hours. I guess they probably don't since they only show up now and then during games. Our next clue comes in and I hop closer to Carlos so he can read it with me.

The best stories provide many twists and turns that lead to a satisfying conclusion. Make your way to this labyrinthine purveyor of books and find the section just for locals.

Carlos groans. "There are at least half a dozen bookstores just in downtown. How are we supposed to know which one it is?"

I grin. "Labyrinthine is the giveaway."

Carlos's eyes fill with hope. "You have the answer?"

"I do."

His arms shoot out and before I know it, he's picked me up and is spinning me around. I laugh at the absurdity. He seems to remember himself and carefully sets me down. "Sorry about that."

I try to temper my smile. All the nerves in my body are lighting up in response to being pressed against Carlos, but I don't want him to know that. The way my body is reacting to his touch has me discombobulated, and until I figure out how I'm feeling, I'd rather keep my turmoil under wraps. "No, it's fine. I'm excited too. We're so close to the end. Only two more to go!"

"Let's finish this thing."

He motions for me to hop on his back. My body tenses in

anticipation of another opportunity to be close to Carlos but, unfortunately, it's not the optimal mode of transportation. I shake my head, hoping the disappointment doesn't show on my face.

"We're going to need a car."

24

Carlos

JUST INSIDE THE door of Page Turner Books, I stop in my tracks and look around. This place is ginormous. I see row after row of shelves filled with books. There are stairs against one wall that lead up to a balcony that heads somewhere. There's no way we're going to find what we're looking for in here. I turn to Abbie and find her watching me.

"Pretty impressive, huh?"

I guess the shock is clear on my face. "I didn't know this store looked like this inside. How have I not been in here before?"

"Like you said, there are quite a few bookstores in town. I know this one because it's where my book club meets."

"You're part of a book club?"

She quirks an eyebrow, obviously offended. "Do I not look like a reader?"

"It's not that. I thought you'd be too busy with your career to commit to a monthly meeting. I've heard how time-consuming and stressful it is being part of college sports. I assume ATs aren't exempt from that?"

She nods. "My sister leads the group, so they understand I'll miss some meetings because of my work schedule, but she thought it might help me meet other people."

"Is she working today?" I look around. "Maybe she can help us find the section we're looking for."

"No need. Follow me."

I look around at the expansive room and make an impulsive decision. I wrap my arms around Abbie's back and legs, picking her up in my arms like I'm about to carry her across a threshold and try not to think about the reason my mind came up with marriage imagery. "This place is way too big for you to hop. Tell me where to go."

Her face reddens. "Put me down. I'll be fine."

I keep my grip on her despite her attempt to twist out of my hold. "No. We still have one more clue before the destination. You've been quite a trooper despite your injury. Anything I can do to help you rest like you should be doing, I'll do."

"Really, Carlos, I can handle it."

My lips curve up slightly, and I shake my head. She's stubborn, but I'm prepared to be more headstrong right now. I saw her wince when she accidentally put too much weight on her foot. She's in more pain than she's been letting on. "We can argue all day, but I thought you wanted to win this thing."

Whatever she was about to say next dies on her tongue. "Fine. Straight ahead."

"Excuse me. Pardon me." People are gracious enough to move out of our way, but we turn plenty of heads and I think I even see a phone pointed in our direction.

"Turn left here. Now take a right down this aisle. All the way to the back."

There's a gigantic mural on the back wall depicting the Blue Ridge Mountains with the city of Asheville in front. In a rainbow across the top, it reads "Local Authors." Shelves dot the wall. There are history books, geography books, and a large section of fiction.

I set Abbie down and move closer to the shelves. The author's name on one book catches my eye. I pull it off the shelf and flip it over. When I see a near replica of Abbie's face smiling back at me, I look up, amazed.

She smiles. "Yep. That's how I knew where this section was. Rachel dragged me over here after her book was published."

"I didn't know your sister is a writer. That's cool."

"I'm pretty proud of her."

"Can I help you find anything?"

I startle, surprised at the man who has appeared at my side. The badge on his shirt tells me his name is Brett. I look up to find him smirking while he swings his gaze between me and Abbie.

"We're fine, Brett," Abbie says, slightly exasperated, which makes me think she knows this guy. "Did Rachel task you with keeping an eye out for me?"

He feigns shock, placing a hand over his heart. "What are you insinuating, Abbie? I'm just a man doing his job of helping people find what they're looking for." He looks over at me. "Though it appears you don't need my help."

Heat rises to Abbie's face. Has this guy hit a little too close to home with his words? She has been slightly less cantankerous towards me today. But maybe this is just wishful thinking on my part.

"Cut it out, Brett. We're kind of on a time crunch here. We

just need a photo and then we'll be out of your hair."

She looks over at me, which feels like my cue. I hand the book to Abbie. "Stand over here and hold up the book for the photo."

"Why don't I take one of the two of you together?" Brett says.

"No, that's okay," Abbie says, but Brett has already snatched the phone out of my hand.

"Okay, you two. Act like you like each other." I stand next to Abbie. "Put your arm around her, man."

I hesitate, not wanting to incur Abbie's wrath from unwanted touching. I've already toed the line carrying by her around in my arms, which I quite enjoyed, and would gladly do some more.

Abbie blows out a breath. "Just do it so he'll take the picture and we can move on."

Lifting my right arm, I wrap my fingers lightly around her shoulder. All I'm touching is her T-shirt, but something about this feels right to me. We smile at Brett's 'say cheese' command, then Abbie sets the book back on the shelf and gives Brett a scowl until he hands over the phone.

"You two look good together," he says before disappearing back into the maze of shelves.

She sends off the photo, not even bothering to look at it. I hold out my arms. "Oh no," she says. "Let's stick with piggy back rides."

I'm a little disappointed. It had felt good holding Abbie against my chest. I felt kind of like a knight protecting his fair lady, though I'd never say that out loud to Abbie. Who knows how she'd react? I turn my back and crouch down. I hear her sigh before she climbs up. I guess she's not enjoying this closeness like I am.

I've really enjoyed reconnecting with her these past two days.

She's smart, determined, flexible, inventive, and resilient. Not to mention gorgeous. I've loved seeing her fight through adversity. She seems to love a challenge just as much as I do. Even as friends, I think we could have a lot of fun together. Not that I want to be just friends. The crush I had on her in high school is nothing compared to the feelings I'm experiencing now. I thought Abbie was awesome then, but she's turned into a feisty and fantastic woman. Of course, she'd probably laugh in my face if I said any of this to her.

I adjust her weight on my back and secure her with my hands. I'd better enjoy these last few moments we have together because once this race is over, who knows if I'll see her again?

Unless we win. Then we'll be the new spokespeople of Asheville tourism and have to do events and commercials together. My heart pounds at the thought. Now I want to win this thing as much for myself as I do to help Abbie get what she wants.

The phone pings in Abbie's hand, and she opens it in front of us. It's our next clue.

This colorful I-240 underpass contains depictions of famous Asheville citizens and the history of Western North Carolina. Focus on the one designed by Molly Must that depicts two players, one of whom was an extra in a movie doing the same thing as the mural.

I walk toward the front of the store. "They must mean the Lexington Avenue Gateway Mural."

"I agree. How far away from here is it?"

"Four or five blocks. I've got this."

A kind person holds the door open for us. I turn left out of the store and take a quick left onto Walnut. I pick up my pace on the downhill, turning left again when we reach North Lexington Avenue. More downhill helps us go even faster. It feels awkward having Abbie bumping against my back, but we're headed toward our last clue before the finish and I want to get there as quickly as possible. A tiny voice in my head reminds me I could be hurtling us toward heartbreak if it turns out we're not the first team to the finish line. I can't think like that. We have seen no one else since The Soda Fountain and we've been doing great on clues, so I feel good about our odds.

We reach the underpass and I set Abbie down in front of the mural of two guys playing chess. I motion for her to hand me the phone, but she shakes her head, grabs my hand, and pulls me to her side. She opens the camera and puts it in selfie mode. Then she wraps her free arm around my waist. "It's our last picture. It should be together like our first one."

I'm tempted to remind her that our last photo was of us together, but wisely, keep my mouth shut. Instead, I put my arm around her shoulders and we lean our heads together. Abbie angles the phone so you can see part of the chessboard and one of the players and then grins. I match her smile. She pushes the button and sends it off. My fingers are itching to grab the phone so I can text that photo to myself.

"Hey, can I see the phone real quick?"

She passes it over. "Sure. What for?"

I'm trying to come up with a reasonable excuse. "Uh, just want to see how much money we have left in case we want to get a snack when we reach our destination. I've depleted all the snacks I took this morning from the table."

"Oh, good idea. My reserve is gone too and my body isn't too happy that it hasn't had proper food since this morning. If you can even call an apple Danish proper food."

I open our wallet since that's what I said I would do. "We've got about thirty dollars. That could buy a couple of burgers or something."

"I'm kind of craving a burrito. Is that weird?"

"No, that sounds good, too. We'll figure something out at the finish."

I close the app and open the photo folder. I quickly send off the pictures we've taken since I last messaged myself. The phone sounds with our last clue and I close the photos, delete the text string with myself, and press the new message. Abbie places her chin on my shoulder and I close my eyes for a second to enjoy the moment. I hold the phone up so we can both read it.

You're almost there. Make your way to the heart of this building rich with history. Opened in 1929, it was closed in 1942 and used by the military for the duration of World War II. In 1951, it became home to the National Weather Records Center, where it remained until it received a new federal building in 1995. Public support grew for the building to return to its original use. In 2002, it reopened once again as a Public Market housing a collection of local shops and services.

A collection of local shops and services gives me the best clue of where we're going, but I'm not completely certain. Maybe Abbie can confirm my guess. "What do you think?"

Abbie removes her chin from my shoulder, and I immediately miss the connection. "I don't know. I guess we should look it up."

"I think it's referencing the Grove Arcade, but I'm not one hundred percent sure. We should be confident before we move."

Abbie takes the phone from my hand. I watch her type "Grove Arcade Asheville" into the search bar of the browser. The first result is the website and there are several options. She clicks on "History" and scrolls down the page.

"Grand opening 1929. Closed during WWII." She looks up at me with wide eyes. "That's enough confirmation for me. Let's go."

I take a second to figure out the best route in my head and then offer her my back. She hops on and I take off.

"How do you know this city so well?" Her voice is choppy because she's being bounced up and down as I move as fast as I can without worrying I'll drop her.

"I've explored most of it in search of ideas and inspiration for my art."

"What kind of art do you make again?"

"Various kinds. Whatever inspires me."

"I can't wait to see your website."

I don't respond because I'm not sure what to say to that. Also, I'm struggling to breathe a bit. Our trek is mostly uphill and my legs are burning, but I'm doing my best not to show any weakness or sign of fatigue because I'm sure Abbie would insist on hopping the rest of the way. We reach the corner of Page Turner Books at the top of the hill and I let out a huff of relief that the next block is downhill before the final uphill push. I can do it. This is for Abbie and possibly a chance at friendship, or maybe even something more. I dig into the last of my energy reserves and force my legs to move faster.

25

Abbie

MY HEART IS pounding by the time we reach the doors to the Grove Arcade. A group exits, and the last person holds them open for us to walk through. I wave thanks to them as Carlos dashes through. He stops just inside the door and I look around for a sign that will tell us where we're going. Up on the left, about fifty feet away, I spot an Amazing Asheville banner, Shannon and Trey, and a bullseye on the floor in front of them.

I point over Carlos's shoulder.

"There it is!"

Carlos turns his head in the direction I'm pointing and then takes off. I feel myself falling back and hook my arm around Carlos's neck. I'm sure my forearm is crushing his windpipe, but he doesn't slow down. Just grunts and keeps moving his feet. We reach the finish mat in a few seconds, both of us silent as we wait for the pronouncement that will tell us if all of our hustling was successful.

Shannon smiles at us. "Abbie and Carlos. Congratulations! You are the second team to reach the finish line."

The words are a shock of ice water to my system. I release my hold on Carlos's neck and slide off his back. I barely notice the pain that radiates from my ankle when I land hard on both feet. We lost. I'm devastated. I want to be mad at Carlos just so I don't have to feel the overwhelming sadness, but I just don't have it in me. It's not his fault. He's been hustling all day. Without his knowledge of the city, there's no way we would have completed all the challenges so quickly. If I'd checked to make sure the phone was charging after I plugged it in, we wouldn't have had a delay this morning. Way to go, Abbie.

Shannon and Carlos are looking at me like they're waiting for me to say something. Oops. "I'm sorry, what?"

"I asked if we can let our race paramedic look at your ankle," Shannon says.

"Oh, uh, it'll be fine," I say, waving her off.

"Actually, it's not really a request. We need to have you checked out before you leave."

"Okay."

She smiles. "Great! After you do that, head down that hall and get some food from our buffet while you wait for the remaining teams to arrive. Don't forget to drop off your race phone at the table and pick up your personal items. Please don't send out any information about the results of the race to family or friends until we've announced the official winner to the group."

Carlos offers me his back, but I shake him off. Without warning, he sweeps me off my feet and carries me over to the staff paramedic. His steady heart pulses against the hand I have pressed against his chest.

"This really isn't necessary," I say.

"I heard the sound you made when you landed on your ankle. You at least need ice, probably more painkillers."

He sets me down on a chair and waits while the paramedic removes the wrap and inspects my ankle. I wince when he presses too firmly on it.

"It's just sprained. Keep it wrapped, elevated as much as you can, add ice, and take some Tylenol."

"Yeah, thanks," I say, too tired to be more polite. I look up at Carlos. "I, uh, didn't hear everything Shannon said. Are we supposed to stay here until all the teams reach the finish line?"

He nods. "When we're all here, they're going to give the official announcement of the winners. Apparently, there are some parting gifts for everyone else."

I can't see his face from this angle, but he sounds as disappointed as I feel. Once my shoe's back on, I grudgingly climb onto his back and he moves us over to a table. The person on the other side holds out their hand and my brow creases.

"I'll take the phone," he says.

I feel foolish. "Right. Here you go. Let me find the charger."

I tap Carlos's shoulder, and he slowly releases me to the ground. Digging through my backpack, I pull out the charger and pass it across the table.

"Thanks. What are your names?"

"Abigail Price and Carlos Vega."

He bends down behind the table. When he stands back up, he's holding plastic bags with our names on them. I toss mine into my backpack. If I'm not supposed to communicate with family and friends, I don't need my phone right now. Carlos opens the bag and sticks his keys, wallet, and phone into his pockets. He locks eyes with me and I'm sure the sadness I see in them is mirrored in mine. We were so close! It wasn't supposed to end this way.

"Should we get something to eat?" he says.

My stomach is queasy from the knowledge that we've lost. Still, it would probably be beneficial to choke something down. "Sure."

I hop over to the buffet, tired of feeling like an invalid from being carried around. We grab plates and lift lids to see what our options are. I'm surprised to find that it's a variety of food from the restaurants in the Arcade. My stomach growls when I smell chicken parmesan from Gli Amanti's sister restaurant, Amore. I put some on my plate along with salad and some penne pasta.

At the end of the row, we pick up drinks and silverware. To the right are a few tables and my eyes meet with those of a guy from another team. They must be the winners because there aren't any other teams around. Jealousy swells up inside me. I try to stomp it back down.

Carlos takes my plate and bottled water from me, then takes a seat at the table right next to them. He shakes their hands, which irritates me. I was hoping to lick my wounds in private, not cozy up next to the people who kept me from victory. Carlos is too nice.

Reluctantly, I hobble over to where the guys are and sit across from Carlos. He taps the seat of the chair next to him until I realize he wants me to prop up my ankle. When I do, he sets a bag of ice wrapped in napkins on top of it. The thoughtfulness of it creates a lump in my throat. My heart swells with affection toward him. Uh oh. I really *do* like him. Though, honestly, what's not to like about someone who looks for the best in everyone, doesn't seem to hold grudges, and is genuinely likable?

"This is Chaz," Carlos says, "and that's Tank. Guys, this is my partner, Abbie."

I pause, caught off guard at being referred to as Carlos's

partner. Why do I kind of wish he meant that in a different way?

"Congratulations on first place." I attempt a smile but know it doesn't reach my eyes.

"Thanks," Tank says. The guys exchange a glance, then both stand up and take their plates to a bin. They sit down at a table farther away and pull out their phones.

"Guess they didn't want to sit with us losers," I mumble under my breath.

Carlos gives me a look, but says nothing. I pick at my food with my fork, but can't stomach more than a few bites. I'm starting to feel hollow inside now that the adrenaline of the race is wearing off.

"I'm sorry we didn't win."

I look up. Carlos is looking at me with eyes that underline the regret in his words. My heart warms with appreciation for his concern.

"Eh. It happens. At least we had fun, right?"

The edges of Carlos's mouth tip up, but not enough for an actual smile.

"Right."

He looks even more dejected than I probably do. I didn't think the prize money meant as much to him as it did to me. Maybe it did. Just because he doesn't lay out a fifteen point plan for achieving his goals like I do, doesn't mean he isn't serious or dedicated to achieving his goal. Not everyone is like me.

His arm is on the table and I reach out and pat his forearm in what I hope is a reassuring gesture.

"I'm sorry your plan of being a full-time artist is going to take longer to achieve."

His whole body shrugs.

"No problemo. I'll get there when it's the right time. I'm sorry you can't get a new car."

I frown. I'd almost forgotten about that. Guess it's back to riding the bus.

"It's not your problem. I'll figure something out."

Carlos straightens, shedding some of the sadness that had enveloped him earlier. "You can use my truck."

I shake my head. "You have to get to work, too."

"I can get a ride from one of my sisters or a co-worker. I live really close to the school."

I hesitate. It would be nice not to have to rely on public transportation, but I can't be in debt to Carlos. He's already done so much for me this weekend. I open my mouth to decline, but he holds up a hand to stop me.

"You're probably going to say that you can't take my offer, but you can. Friends help friends. We are friends now, right?"

After these past two days, how can I not consider him a friend? Though, the thought of us only being friends is suddenly disappointing. I nod, which elicits a genuine smile from him. It gives me a jolt of satisfaction. Why does making Carlos smile feel so good?

"Then, as my friend, please take my truck until you can figure something out."

I sigh. "Fine."

He stands up, which catches me off guard. "I'm going to get some more to eat. Want anything?"

I look down at my still nearly full plate. "Nah, I'm good."

He heads back to the buffet. I put down my fork. I'm clearly not going to eat anything else. I reach down for my bag and pull out my phone. Might as well see what I've missed these past two days. I have a couple of encouraging messages from my family, but I don't respond because I'm not sure what I'm allowed to say yet.

I send Carlos a text with a link to my website before I forget and decide to look for his website on my own. I type in *Carlos Vega art.* I click on the first link, which takes me to an About the Artist page on a website. There's a photo of him which doesn't do him justice. He should get some official headshots. I scan through the article. It talks about his time at Savannah College of Art and Design, his job at W. B. Hines Elementary School, and how he finds inspiration in nature, especially the Blue Ridge Mountains.

I click on the home button and freeze when I see the logo at the top of the page. It's two rainbows with the words Double Rainbow Designs underneath. The clink of his plate hitting the table draws my eye up to Carlos. He sits down in the chair and picks up his fork, but pauses when he sees me staring.

"What? Do I have food on my face?" He grabs a napkin and wipes the lower half of his face. "Did I get it?"

I blink out of my stupor. "*You're* Double Rainbow Designs?"

He looks away and rubs the back of his neck. "Yeah, I am."

My mind floods with the memory of me gushing about his art. *To him.* I'm embarrassed, but it comes out as anger. "Why didn't you tell me?"

He leans back when I fire the words at him. "I'm sorry?"

I scowl. "You let me wax poetic about your work and didn't say anything."

He smiles, which only irritates me more. "I mean. It was nice to hear you saying something nice about me for a change. I didn't want to ruin the art for you."

His words sting me, and I deflate a little. I was pretty rude to him. "I'm sorry about that. And for being so mean and unforgiving about the prom thing. I know you were just trying to look out for my sister. I have a tendency to think poorly of others and hold a grudge longer than is warranted. It's definitely something I need to work on."

He nods. "You're protective of your family. I understand. Having three younger sisters, I am too."

His graciousness feels undeserved. "You really are a very talented artist. I hope you get to make art full-time."

"And I hope everything works out with your situation. I want you to succeed and have everything your heart desires."

Why is he being so nice to me? He doesn't seem to let anything bother him. Maybe he could teach me to be a little more like that. His warm gaze is doing weird things to my insides and I break eye contact. I pull up my email as cover. I have one from the Athletic Director, sent yesterday morning. I read it and my stomach drops. Sweat breaks out on my skin and it's suddenly hard to breathe. I'm panting, trying to get air into my lungs. My eyes search wildly for I don't know what and lock onto Carlos's.

His brow crinkles and his eyes widen. His fork clatters against his plate. "Abbie? What's wrong?"

26

Carlos

I STAND UP so fast, my chair scrapes against the floor. I rush around the table, place a hand on Abbie's back, and rub in a circle. She shrugs me off, and I take a step away from her.

"Abbie, breathe with me. In for three and out for three."

Her eyes are wild with panic, and I hold out my hand. She grabs it and squeezes. I try not to wince, but apply steady pressure against her iron grip, hoping to help ground her.

"Can you breathe in through your nose and release it through your mouth?"

Her eyes narrow slightly and it looks like she's trying to glare at me, but she's still too worked up.

"Yes," she huffs out.

I nod and keep my voice calm and steady, despite the concern causing my heart to thrash.

"Good. With me. In, two, three and out, two, three. You've

got this. I'm here with you. Don't worry. We'll do this together."

I continue to hold her gaze, happy when the alarm in her expression recedes. Her shoulders drop from her ears and her chest expands with a lungful of air. She slowly exhales through her lips, and it seems like her body is returning to normal. I give her a reassuring squeeze of the hand that's still in mine. It seems to register that we're holding hands, and she releases her grip. My arm falls back to my side. "How are you feeling?"

She looks away, color tingeing her cheeks. "Better, thanks. Sorry about that."

"You have nothing to apologize for."

She brushes a hand over her hair. "How did you know what I needed?"

I give her what I hope is a disarming smile. "One of my sisters gets panic attacks sometimes."

She looks up, surprised, but keeps her lips pressed together. I'm curious to know what brought hers on, but I don't want to be intrusive. I look around the space and notice more brightly colored competition shirts. I count the different teams.

"Looks like we're only two teams short. Or maybe just one. I don't know which team got eliminated yesterday. They might still have to be here for the finale. Regardless, hopefully, they'll show up soon and we can all get out of here."

"Ready to get away from me, are you?" Her voice is teasing, but there's a hint of something else. Hurt, maybe?

"No, just tired. And I feel pretty gross wearing the same clothes two days in a row."

She wrinkles her nose. "You and me both."

It's kind of awkward having a conversation when I'm standing and she's sitting, so I move back around the table, sit down, and take a bite of food, though I'm no longer hungry. I set my fork down and push my plate away. I cast around in my brain for a new conversation topic, but blurt out what's on my mind. "Is everything okay?"

She sighs and slumps against the chair. "No. I got an email from my boss. He wants to see me tomorrow for a meeting with HR."

"That sounds a little ominous."

She crosses her arms across her chest. "I know. We've had some interpersonal conflict, but not enough that HR needs to be involved. Unless he's firing me."

I lean forward, my body straightening to attention. "Do you really think that's what this is about?"

Abbie lifts a shoulder. "I hope not, but I can't think of what else it could be. Looks like I might not need your truck after all."

I reach across the table and take her hand again. I'm surprised when she doesn't pull away but try not to show it. "Don't say that. It doesn't do any good to think the worst."

She looks over my head and is quiet for a few seconds. "I suppose you're right. Worrying about it won't change anything. It's just another heap on the pile of disappointment that is today."

My heart twists in sympathy. I hate how this day has turned out. Yes, it started out pretty terrible, but we really turned it around. It was one of the best days I've had in a while, actually. "I'm sorry. I doubt this helps, but I really enjoyed having you as my race partner."

She gives me a skeptical look. "Really? You enjoy being yelled at and criticized?"

I smile wryly. "Well, maybe some parts were less than great, but overall, I had fun. I thought we made a good team."

She considers this and then nods. "Yeah, you're right. Where one was weak, the other was strong."

I flex my biceps and wink. "Literally."

A chuckle escapes from her. "I felt kind of like a princess being rescued when you carried me through the bookstore. Definitely a first for me."

I'm a little sad no one's made her feel like royalty before. "I think you deserve to be treated like a queen. You're smart, resourceful, determined, beautiful, tough, and strong."

"And stubborn, judgmental—"

I silence her with a finger to her lips. "Can't you just take the compliment?"

It takes me a second to realize what I'm doing. The softness of her lips against my skin fills my brain with thoughts of kissing her. My heart pangs with a longing to give in to the impulse. Abbie seems to register it at almost the same time because her eyes round like saucers. I quickly remove my finger from her oh-so-kissable pink lips. My pulse has kicked up at the intimacy of the situation and Abbie is blushing. Is she feeling what I'm feeling?

"You're right," she says after a few silent beats between us. "Thank you. You're not so bad yourself."

"Wow, an almost-compliment from my former enemy. My day is made."

She laughs.

"Attention Amazing Asheville competitors." Our heads snap over to Trey. "All teams have arrived at the finish line. Please make your way to the finish line, where we will announce the results."

I turn back to Abbie, who looks nervous. "I guess it's time."

Abbie grabs her backpack, and I remove the ice pack from her ankle so she can stand up. I grab our plates and clear the table. When I return to her side, I turn and offer her my back.

"I think I can manage," she says.

This may be my last chance to be close to her. I have to take it. "Why just manage when you have someone willing to help you with your burden? It's either a piggy back ride or the princess carry."

She sighs, but it seems more wistful than affronted. She sets her hands on my shoulders and hops onto my back. I steady her with my hands, savoring the feel of her warm body against mine. As soon as we're in the crowd with the rest of the teams, she taps my shoulder. I set her down and turn my gaze to Trey and Shannon so I don't do something impulsive like lace my fingers with hers.

"Thank you all for participating in this fun competition, which we hope will show a new side of Asheville and spark the interest of potential visitors. Did you enjoy the race around town?"

People nod in response, and one person shouts "yeah" so enthusiastically, I chuckle. I glance around and see smiles on quite a few tired faces. I'm sure we're all looking forward to a shower and a good night's sleep.

"As you know, the rules of the competition were clear. Each team must visit the location and either take a photo or complete a challenge before moving on. After some research, we've discovered some cheating."

A surprised murmur passes through the group and someone raises their hand. "What kind of cheating?"

"Photos from the internet were used to check in rather than actually going to the location and taking a picture per the regulations."

Tank raises his hand. "How can you tell? Maybe some of us have amazing photography skills."

"Besides the photos being identical to images found from a web search, the log from the car rider app confirmed our suspicions."

A third hand shoots up. Chaz, Tank's partner. "Maybe they walked to the locations."

Trey shakes his head. "One photo in question was the chess set at Biltmore Estate. There's no record of the team ordering a car to drop them off or pick them up. If they'd walked, they wouldn't have finished the competition as quickly as they did."

Was it just one team that cheated or several? I glance around, but there aren't any guilty looks on the surrounding faces. I look at Abbie, but she's focused on the coordinators. I wonder what's going through her head. She's probably indignant about the fact that someone cheated. She doesn't seem like someone who'd take shortcuts even if they weren't illegal.

"Those who were involved will not be named. It isn't our desire to shame anyone. We understand that the competition prize is very enticing, however we don't condone cheating. All that being said, we'd now like to announce the winners of the race and our new Asheville spokespeople. When we call your names, please come forward."

Trey pushes something on his phone, and we hear a quiet drum roll. There's a nervous chuckle from the group.

"Our winners of the Amazing Asheville Race are…Abbie and Carlos!"

My mouth drops open and I turn to see an identical dazed expression on Abbie's face. We won? I break out of my stunned stupor first. I grab Abbie and pull her to me. "We won!"

The jolt seems to restart her brain, and she throws her arms around my neck and squeezes. I try to kiss her on the cheek, but she moves her head at the same time and our lips touch. Their softness and warmth draw me closer to her until I realize what's happening. I jerk my head back, but there's still the phantom feel of Abbie's lips on mine. I will replay this moment in my head for a long time. Her arms release their hold on my neck, and I feel her hands press firmly against my chest. That's an obvious sign for 'get away from me' if I've ever seen one.

"Sorry, so sorry," I blurt, releasing my arms and taking a step back.

She presses a hand to her mouth and looks away. "Uh, we'd better head up front."

I cannot believe that just happened. I've wanted to kiss Abbie most of the weekend, but I didn't intend for it to happen by accident or in a group of strangers. Any chance of us ever being more than friends has just gone up in flames. I follow Abbie up to the front of the group, feeling about three inches tall.

This does not bode well for the future. We are now officially are part of a campaign together. My dream has come true, but now it feels more like a nightmare. How am I going to be able to work with her when all I'm going to be thinking of are her lips and how much I want to kiss her again? But I can't. She obviously doesn't feel the way I do. Maybe she knows it was an accident. All I can do is send up a prayer that she doesn't think I did it on purpose.

27

Abbie

I FOLLOW CARLOS up to the front of the group. He stands to the left of Trey and I stop on the right side of Shannon. Trey frowns and moves everyone around so that Carlos and I are now between the two of them, our arms touching. I can't look at Carlos right now. My brain's still trying to sort out everything that happened in the last thirty seconds.

We won the competition, which is an incredible surprise. Carlos and I both know we came in second, which means the first-place team definitely cheated. I admire the coordinators for not wanting to let everyone know what really happened. I don't know that I would be as level-headed if I found out about cheating. I've been very firm with all the players I've worked with that they need to do everything the right way so there won't be anything that could hold them back from what they want to achieve.

When Carlos pulled me into a hug, it felt so natural. I have begun to appreciate the feel of his muscles under my hands and against my chest. I hadn't known until today that piggy back rides were so enjoyable. Maybe I just needed the right back to lean on. And what a back he has. And biceps, and stomach, and face. Absently, I turn my head to glance at him. Carlos looks pained, like he's carrying some regret. Okay, so maybe the kiss was a surprise to him, too. I suppose it could have been an accident. A very enjoyable accident.

Carlos notices me staring at him, frowns, and looks away. What does that mean? Did our kiss repulse him? *Oh, Abbie, did you have the idea that he still likes you? Why would someone like him still harbor feelings for you? He obviously has no problem attracting women, as he clearly showed while working for tips earlier today. He's a kind, considerate, gentle soul. He's nothing like you who thinks the worst of others and is quick to judge.*

I sigh. My conscience is right. My eyes widen in horror. What if he thinks I kissed him on purpose and is trying to let me down gently? I need to straighten this out ASAP. I definitely didn't mean for it to happen, but I can't deny the way my body reacted to it. The jolt was so strong; it felt like I'd touched an electric fence. My lips are still tingling from where they were pressed against his. I haven't ever felt anything like that when I've kissed someone else. Maybe it was just the buildup of tension from this whole crazy weekend. Yeah, that's probably it. Part of me wants to do it again to see if I'd feel the same powerful sensations. For research purposes, of course. Though the look on Carlos's face makes it seem like that isn't going to happen.

"How do you know *they* didn't cheat?"

My head snaps over to the part of the crowd where the question came from. I narrow my eyes when I see it's Tank who made the remark.

"Their app log shows rides to all the locations that were too far to walk from the previous clue," says Trey, unfazed.

Chaz pipes up. "That doesn't mean they actually went to all the places. They could have skipped the close ones. All the downtown buildings have plenty of photos online."

Shannon rolls her eyes.

"Every photo they sent has at least one of them in it."

"They could have photoshopped themselves into the pictures."

These guys don't know when to quit.

Trey shakes his head. "We considered that possibility and had a photography expert check the authenticity. Abbie and Carlos are our winners. End of discussion."

He reaches behind a table and pulls out a big check with our names on it. I laugh, uncomfortably. I did not care for the attack on our integrity, but Shannon and Trey handled it like a pro. Now I'm super grateful Carlos insisted one of us be in each photo. I have the urge to touch him, maybe squeeze his hand to express my gratitude, but if he were to pull away from me in front of all of these people, I'd be mortified.

I keep my hands to myself until I need them to hold up the cardboard rectangle Trey gives us. A photographer appears in front of us and tells us to smile. The camera clicks a few times and then the giant rectangle is taken away and we're handed manila envelopes.

"Okay, competitors," Shannon says. "That's it for the Amazing Asheville race. Thank you for participating. Trey will give you the gift bags for participating. You are free to go and welcome to tell others about your experience."

I take a step forward, but a hand on my shoulder makes me pause. I look over at Shannon.

"We still need to tell you two a few more things. The big check is just for show. Your money will be deposited directly into your accounts tomorrow. The packets have information about shooting the commercials and public appearances."

She smiles brightly at both of us. "We look forward to working together. You two will be fantastic. We'll probably use some of the photos you took in the promotion. They were so fun!"

Carlos is the first one of us to speak.

"Is there anything else we need to do now? Who do we contact if we have questions?"

"You're good for today. Contact information for both Trey and myself is in the envelope. Someone will contact you both next week to coordinate schedules for the first commercial."

Carlos nods. "Thanks." He turns and looks at me. "How are you getting home?"

"Rachel said she'd come get me."

Carlos glances at his phone. "It's kind of late. Why don't I just take you?"

He is so thoughtful and kind, it's killing me. "I'm sure you're more than ready for a break from me. Rachel won't mind."

He sucks in his lips and sighs. "Why are you so stubborn?"

His words make my hackles rise, but I'm too tired to really argue, so I just shrug. "Born that way, maybe?"

"Look, it won't take me long to run home and grab my truck. Please let me drive you. Then you'll have my truck for work tomorrow."

It's hard to argue with that logic. "Fine. I'll go with you to save time."

He holds up a hand.

"No. Sit down, prop up your ankle, and wait. You don't need to risk putting any more unnecessary pressure on it today."

I'm touched by his concern. It's probably because we bonded a little as teammates today. Nothing more. "Okay. I'll wait."

Without a word, he scoops me up into his arms and carries me out of the Arcade's front doors. My arm is pressed against his firm chest, and I have the urge to run my hand across it. I don't, because I still have a small amount of control, but with our faces so close together, I can see he has hazel eyes. I'd thought they were just brown, but there's definitely some green and amber mixed in. My gaze tracks down his face and snags on his lips. His electrifying lips. If I just leaned forward a couple of inches, I could kiss the corner of his mouth. I wonder what he'd do. I know this isn't a good idea and tear my eyes away from his face before I do something I'll regret. He sets me down gently on a bench on the sidewalk, carefully extending my injured leg out along the seat.

"Be back in a flash."

He jogs down the sidewalk away from me, and I can't help but watch his backside as he recedes. I sigh. He's just so perfect. He's considerate and kind, even to people he doesn't care that much about. And I love the way he can effortlessly carry me around. It makes me feel feminine, something I don't get a lot of with my job. At the school, I'm definitely seen and treated like one of the guys, which is great, but I'm still a woman and it's nice to feel seen that way once in a while. And Carlos definitely makes me feel like a woman.

I shake my head. *Get yourself together, Abs. He's just a nice guy. He doesn't like you like that.*

I still can't believe I didn't know Carlos liked me in high school. Probably because he flirted with all the girls. That's just the way he was. If I'd had any inkling that he'd actually been interested in me, I'd...what? What would I have done? If it had been before prom, maybe I could have convinced him to just tell Rachel that

Ryan was a creep. And maybe we would have gone to prom together and kissed at the end of the night.

My mind floats back to our kiss earlier and I touch my mouth when I remember how soft Carlos's lips felt against mine. It's been awhile since I've dated, but I don't remember any other kisses feeling like that. Almost like there was a current running between us. It's probably all in my head. I'm tired and physically exhausted and injured. On cue, my ankle throbs. I fish two pills out of my bag and swallow them.

Carlos really was so considerate of my ankle today. He's so lovely and thoughtful. I'm definitely into him.

The thought makes me pause. I'm what now? Surely not. I mean, yes, he's very good looking and has a body I could stare at all day. And sure, he's been so good to me these past two days, brushing off my harsh comments and doing whatever he can to help us win.

That power pack was pure genius. I can't believe he bartered his work for it. His art is worth so much more than whatever a phone battery costs.

And his art! Oh my goodness, it's so beautiful. I can't believe I have one of his mountains in my house. His work is so incredible and inspired. How does he still have to work two jobs to support himself? I hope that isn't the situation for too much longer because I'd love to see what he can make when it's his sole focus. One question plagues me. How did he decide on the name Double Rainbow Designs? It doesn't really seem to fit him.

A truck pulls up to the sidewalk. Carlos gets out of the driver's side and walks around the front. He stops in front of me and grins widely. My lips curve up and my eyes crinkle in automatic response. My heart picks up its pace and my body leans forward like it wants to be closer to him. And then it hits me. I *really* like

Carlos. A lot.

He bends down and lifts me off the bench. My skin crackles with energy at the physical contact and I suck in a deep breath. I smell something woodsy which is new. And also very enjoyable. I turn my head toward his neck and breathe in again through my nose. It's definitely Carlos who smells so good. How is that possible after two days of competition? He must be magic.

My stomach feels fluttery and warning bells are clanging in my head. This drive home is going to be torture, but surely I can keep my newly realized feelings for him under wraps for another few minutes. At least while I'm sitting with him in his truck cab as he chivalrously goes out of his way to make sure I get home okay. I close my eyes and groan internally. This may be harder than I think.

28

Carlos

I CARRY ABBIE over to the car and realize my mistake. I should have opened the door before retrieving her. I stop walking and consider my options. I can set her down, open the door, and then help her in again, but that ruins the smooth guy vibe I'm trying to portray. I could see if I could reach the handle while holding her, but I might accidentally press her up against the side of the truck and I can't guarantee she won't get dirt on her. Of course, neither of us are all that clean after two days in the same shirt, but still.

Abbie decides for me by leaning over and opening the door from her position in my arms. Duh, Carlos. I maneuver around the open door and set her gently inside on the seat.

"Thanks for getting the door."

She smiles, catches my eye, and immediately looks away again. "Thanks for being so considerate."

I shake my head. "It's no problem at all."

I shut the passenger door, walk around to the other side, and climb in behind the steering wheel. I fish my phone out of my pocket, open a navigation app, and hand it out to Abbie. "Will you put in your address for me, please?"

She hands my phone back after I buckle my seatbelt. I stick it to the magnet on my dash. It's only a seven-minute drive to her house and my stomach sinks at the realization that our time together is almost up. Though, obviously after our accidental kiss, I'm also glad that I have little chance of doing something else dumb. Above all else, I cannot let her know I still have feelings for her. A kiss is one thing, but adding in emotions would definitely scare her off for good. I try to come up with a safe topic, but Abbie speaks up first.

"Are you wearing cologne?"

Did I put too much on that she can smell it from her side of the truck? It hasn't slipped my notice that she's pressed herself up against the door. She looks ready to make a quick escape as soon as we reach her place. Maybe she's trying to get away from the smell of me.

"It's body spray. I could smell myself when I first hopped into the truck and thought you might prefer not to smell my body odor. I usually keep deodorant and body spray in the car in case I don't have time to shower after a basketball game. Is it too strong? I can roll down the windows."

She shakes her head. "No. It smells nice. I was just wondering what it is."

I'm relieved and a little pleased to know that she likes it. "It's called Rustic Woods."

"It suits you. Of course, now I'm worried that you can smell my body odor."

She unzips her backpack and rummages around, coming up

with a stick of deodorant. She lifts her shirt to apply it and I catch a sliver of stomach. My eyes don't want to tear themselves away, but I force them to return to the front window.

"You smell fine to me. So, I guess first up on your agenda is finding a new car."

She smiles. "I guess so. It's still sinking in that we won. I'm so glad you insisted that one of us be in the photos. How did you know?"

Her words feel like a lifeline. Maybe our renewed friendship is going to survive the kiss mishap. "I think pictures are more interesting when there are people in them. I didn't know it would be so important."

She reaches over and squeezes my forearm, but quickly removes her hand and retreats to her side of the car. Her smile disappears and lines crease her forehead. What just happened? "Hey, Abbie, is everything okay?"

She sighs. "Yes. No. I don't know. I just started thinking about that email from work."

My lips thin out and my forehead creases with worry. "Maybe it's not as serious as you're thinking. It won't change anything to worry. Tell me about what else you might do with your money."

She sits up a little straighter. "Actually, my sister and I talked about taking a trip together if I won."

Now that sounds like a good thing to do with prize money. Maybe I should take a trip as well. "Oh yeah? Where to?"

Her cheeks fill with color. "We were thinking Puerto Rico."

I smile. "I think that's a great idea. Why there?"

She turns her head to stare out the front windshield. "The food, actually. Rachel loved the rice your mom made at the family gathering and thought it'd be fun to get some from the source."

I laugh. "Man, if my mom hears that her cooking inspired a

trip to Puerto Rico, she'll be over the moon."

"Feel free to tell her."

"If I do, just know that you'll be forced to go home with a Tupperware filled with rice every time you see her."

Abbie grins. "That sounds like a win-win situation to me."

It makes me supremely happy to hear Abbie likes my mom's cooking. An image of us together at a family gathering, me with an arm slung casually around her waist, enters my mind and I have to shake my head to dislodge it. That's never going to happen. She's just happy because she's still on a high from winning. I'm under no pretense that she sees me as anything but her race partner. I wish there was some way for her to give me a chance, but it's just a fantasy of my mind.

"So, what are you going to do with your share of the money?"

Her question brings me back to reality. "I actually haven't seriously thought about it. I'd always considered it a vague notion, like winning the lottery. Fun to speculate, but never with an intention of concrete plans. Though, I probably should have given it more thought once I knew we were partners. Of course you were going to win."

She appears pleased by my words. "You'd mentioned something about quitting teaching. Is that still a possibility?"

I'm a little surprised she remembers that conversation. I didn't figure she really cared about my own interests or ambitions. Or, at least, not for more than just criticizing my lack of a proper plan.

"I mean, I guess. There are only a few more weeks of school and then I have summer break. I'll see how my art sells over the next few months. That'll tell me if I can truly make a go of it full-time."

She leans toward me slightly, which I take as a good sign. "Do you know how much you'd need to make each month to pay bills, buy supplies, and all that?"

I shake my head. "I haven't done the math yet."

She scowls and opens her mouth, but then closes it again. She takes a deep breath, then turns back to me. "If you wanted, I could help you work on that, see what it would really take. I'm pretty good at making an action plan."

My first thought is to say no. I can only imagine how frustrated she'd get with me when she sees how disorganized I am with all of that. But then it hits me she's offering to do something that would require us to spend more time together, which I'd very much like. Though it's only in a business associate type capacity. Still, it's more time with Abbie, which will be a mix of torture and pleasure because of my feelings for her.

"If you don't mind, I would appreciate that. Every time I think about it, I decide to put it off. It's so technical and businessy and I much prefer the creative, fun part."

Abbie chuckles. "Yeah, I can understand that. I'll look at my schedule and we can find a time to meet."

I try not to smile too big. "I definitely need time to get everything together. I don't have a filing system or anything."

Her sigh tells me she's probably already regretting offering to help me. "I'll send you a list of what to put together."

Of course she will. I'm not offended. "That would be a great help, thanks."

She nods. "You're welcome."

There's a lull in the conversation and my mind once again searches for something to say. Once again, Abbie fills the void first. "Did you hear back about that piece you nearly killed yourself finishing up?"

I'm surprised she remembered. Though, I guess my lack of

sleep did nearly blow the race for us, so it'd be hard for her to forget. "Yeah, actually. I had an email from the customer who was very pleased with how it turned out. She said her parents loved it and that a few of the guests asked for my contact info."

Her smile cracks something inside of me. "Carlos, that's so wonderful! Do you think you'll get some more commissions, then?"

I nod. "I received two emails this afternoon from people at the party asking for their own custom pieces."

Abbie squeezes my shoulder, and heat radiates out from her touch. "That's awesome. I'm so happy for you. Your dream is coming true!"

I can't hold back a cheek-stretching smile anymore. "I know. I'm so excited. I'm definitely going to need your help to get organized into an official, functional business."

Her hand slides from my shoulder, down to my forearm, but she doesn't let go. I try to keep my torso as still as possible as I make the last few turns to her apartment to keep it there. This feels like progress in our relationship and I don't want to do anything to ruin it.

29

Abbie

CARLOS PULLS UP to the front of my apartment building. I should be exhausted, but I feel like I've gotten a second wind and am not yet ready for my time with Carlos to end. Our conversation in the car was surprisingly normal. I thought things would be pretty awkward after our kiss, but he seems to have moved on, so I will, too. I've actually come to enjoy his company in this short time we've been together.

Carlos puts the car in park and shuts off the engine, but doesn't open his door. Is this a sign he's reluctant to end our time together as well? He turns, his eyes focusing on my hand, which is resting on his arm. I know immediately that I've been touching him longer than necessary and drop my hand. The current that felt like it was flowing into my hand from his arm is severed, and I immediately want it back.

"I guess I should head inside. We've both had a busy

weekend."

Carlos unbuckles his seatbelt and opens his door. Is he planning to walk me to my door like an actual date? My pulse quickens at the idea. "You don't have to see me to my door."

He pauses, one foot already on the ground. He turns back to look at me. "My truck sits kind of high. I don't want you putting too much weight on your ankle."

Oh, of course. My injury. I'd nearly forgotten. I'm touched by his thoughtfulness. I suppose I could let him help me one last time. Truthfully, I'll take any excuse for the chance to touch him right now. "Okay, thanks."

Carlos comes around to my side of the truck. He opens the door, then slides one arm around my back and the other under my thighs. He's planning to carry me to the door? Heat spreads through my body from our touch points. Might as well take full advantage of this. I hook my backpack over one shoulder and clutch the back of his neck with the arm not pinned against his chest. The closely shaved hair tickles my palm and I rub up and down the back of his head, enjoying the sensations of the short strands on my hand. He clears his throat and my hand freezes. Embarrassment blossoms in my chest. *Get a hold of yourself, Abbie.*

Carlos carries me up to my door and sets me down gently so I can find my key. I open the door and turn back to him. "While you're here, would you like to see which art piece of yours I have?"

His eyes widen a little and his lips part slightly. "Why not?"

That's not very enthusiastic, but I'll take it. There's a small flicker of hope that if he comes in, something may happen. What, I'm not sure. All I know is I'm not ready to let him go just yet. "Follow me."

I hop into the entryway, down a short hallway, past the kitchen, and into the living room. The couch and loveseat face a television, and the coffee table is clean. There's a shelf on the wall behind the couch with a plant and the mountain sculpture I bought several months ago. I wave my hand to the wall. "There she is."

Carlos stops behind me, close enough to feel his body heat on my back. "She?"

I turn around. Only a few inches separate us from one another. I try to grin confidently, but I inhale that woodsy scent again and feel a little lightheaded. "Y-yeah. Mountains seem feminine to me."

Carlos is staring into my eyes, a serious look on his face. He swallows, then takes a step back and my heart sinks. *Pull yourself together. He's made it clear he's not into you. Stop torturing yourself.* Time to find an innocuous topic.

"So, why the name Double Rainbow Designs? Mountain Design seems more appropriate based on what I've seen of your work."

He looks over to the sculpture on the shelf and is silent for so long I wonder if he's going to answer. I should just thank him for being kind and let him get out of here like he so obviously wants to do. "You don't have to answer that. If you need to go, please don't let me keep you."

His face ripples with indecision. After what feels like an eternity, he sighs and swings his gaze back to me. "You should sit down and put your ankle up."

He guides me over to the couch and helps me get comfortable before disappearing into the kitchen. He returns with a bag of ice wrapped in a towel and puts it on my ankle. "Do you need more pain medication?"

I shake my head. "I'm good, thanks."

He hesitates for a second before lowering himself down onto the couch near my propped up leg. He takes a deep breath and then looks me in the eye. My heart stutters and I'm nervous about whatever is coming because his look is so intense. This is it. He's going to let me down easy. Tell me we can be friends, but he doesn't think of me as anything more.

"I named the business after those socks you always used to wear. These socks, I guess."

He gestures at his own legs that are still clad in my socks. I'm confused. "Why would you name your business after my socks?"

He sighs. "You're really going to make me say it, aren't you?"

What is he talking about? My confusion must be obvious from my face, because he shakes his head. He places a hand on my shin and I flinch at the electricity that zings up my leg. He must interpret my reaction as pain because he quickly removes it and drops it in his lap.

"I told you yesterday that I had a crush on you in high school. Well, I never completely got over it. When I saw you at my parents' house the other week, my feelings for you flared back up. These past two days have been so much fun with you."

I'm stunned at his admission, but scoff at his last statement. "I'm sure it was so much fun having me yell at you and talk down to you."

He stands up, looking hurt, and I place a hand on his arm to stop him. I rush my words to keep him from bolting out the front door.

"Carlos, I'm so sorry I was such a jerk. You didn't deserve any of my bad behavior toward you this weekend. You've been nothing but kind to me. Please forgive me."

He nods, but refuses to look at me. I have to say something else to clear the awkwardness hanging in the air. I use his arm to hoist myself up to standing and turn him toward me. He looks over my shoulder. Maybe it'll be easier if he's not looking directly at me.

"I'm very flattered to be the inspiration for your business, but don't feel like I deserve it. You're so considerate and laid back and I'm very intense. We're like oil and water."

I feel him go rigid under my hand.

"Yeah, I get it. We're too different. Thanks for not sugar coating it for me."

What? That's not what I meant at all.

"Carlos, no. I'm trying to say that I appreciate our differences. I think it was an asset for us in the race. Your strengths are my weaknesses. I'm saying we really do make a good team."

He finally looks at me. His forehead is crinkled with doubt.

"Okaaaay…?"

I sigh. What can I do to get through to him?

"Despite our rocky start and bumps along the way, I had a blast being your teammate. Thank you so much for not giving up on me. I think you're an amazing artist and I hope you never stop creating. The world needs the beauty you form from wire and paint."

He still looks doubtful, so I decide to do what feels natural and take a step forward, trying not to wince with the weight on my hurt ankle, and wrap my arms around his neck, closing the remaining space between us. I squeeze him hard and feel his arms loosely circle my waist. Disappointment lances through me. This feels like a goodbye hug, so I hold on a little longer, trying to memorize how he feels against me. His arms tighten against my back and a zap of pleasure races up my spine.

I nuzzle my nose against his neck and breathe in the scent that will always connect me with this moment. My lips tingle with the urge to press against his throat. Instead, I loosen my grip and pull back a bit. My hands rest on Carlos's shoulders and his move to my hips. There's a pull low in my belly and I draw my eyes up to his. His lids are lowered slightly, and his gaze appears to be on my chin. I'm not sure whether it's fatigue or something else. My lips still tingle with want and I drag my tongue across them to ease the sensation.

Something sparks inside Carlos's eyes. My eyes dart down to his mouth. Desire to press my lips against his floods through me. I meet his gaze again and there's a question in them that causes my stomach to squeeze with desire. Is he waiting for me to do something? Our arms are still around each other, so it seems like he's into whatever's happening. Should I just go for it? *Come on, Abbie, make a decision and act. You're usually much better at going for what you want.*

Thanks, inner Abbie. That was just the pep talk I needed. Go big or go home, right? I lean in and tilt my head slightly. Carlos's nostrils flair slightly and then he closes the distance between us until it's nonexistent. All thoughts fly from my head when his mouth presses firmly against mine. I pull his shoulders toward me before letting go to grab the back of his neck in one hand and pulling him against me with the other. One of his hands slides up my back to cradle the back of my head, the other still pressing into the small of my back.

The contentment I initially felt has morphed into a small flame and I tilt my head a little more to deepen the kiss. My whole body ignites, stealing my breath. Carlos must feel it because he breaks the kiss and pulls back a little.

I'm immediately self-conscious, drop my hands, and look away. "Sorry about that. I probably should have asked first. I didn't mean to force myself on you."

He turns my face to his with a gentle hand. "No apologies. I wanted to kiss you."

He gives me a disarming smile, and I relax. He leans forward and gives me a soft peck on the lips, which only fans the flame inside my body. I launch myself at him off of my good ankle. It catches him by surprise and there's a note of panic when I knock him off balance. He wraps his arms around me and tenses his body for hitting the ground. When he lands on the soft couch, he chuckles and adjusts me so I'm comfortably supported on his lap. His eyes beckon me closer and I lean in for another kiss.

30

Carlos

I CAN'T BELIEVE I'm sitting in Abbie Price's house. It's blowing my mind that she's sitting in my lap and we're kissing. If someone had told me last week that this was even a remote possibility, I'd have laughed in their face. And yet, here we are. This is very real and I'm ecstatic.

I'm enjoying the moment immensely, so it's a real mood killer when doubt whispers into my mind that perhaps this is just her getting swept up in the excitement of winning the competition and that she'll regret kissing me tomorrow. My heart squeezes at the thought. I have to know if this is a one-time thing or the beginning of something real so I can manage my expectations.

I break our kiss and lean back into the couch so I can see Abbie's face. "I have to know. What are we doing here?"

Her eyes widen. "You think this is a mistake?"

My stomach twists uncomfortably. Is she reflecting her

thoughts on me or genuinely asking? This is my opportunity to be honest. If I don't take it, I'll always wonder what might have happened if I did. I swallow down the lump in my throat. "No, I don't. I really like you, Abbie. I'd love to date you, if it's something you also want."

My unvarnished honesty seems to catch her off guard. Her lips form a thin line. "I have to admit that this," she motions between us, "surprised me. I've spent so long hating you I doubted that would ever change."

I don't like the sound of that, but at least I gave it a shot. "Okay—"

Abbie claps a hand over my mouth. "Let me finish, please."

I nod, my stomach churning. This won't be pleasant, but I can endure it.

"Like I said, I thought we'd always be enemies after what you did to my sister. But we're not eighteen anymore. You've changed, I've changed. And I really like the man you've become. You're considerate, kind, and resourceful."

I straighten up in my seat. This doesn't sound like an "it's not you, it's me" speech.

"I think we worked well together this weekend," she continues. "I would be interested in spending more time with you, but I have to warn you that my work doesn't allow a ton of time for socializing. I have long hours and an erratic schedule during basketball season. Do you think you could handle that?"

The vulnerability in her eyes fills my heart with compassion. I'm honored by her willingness to open up to me. This is a promising sign for our future. I give what I hope is a reassuring smile.

"Thank you for being honest with me. I can handle a wonky schedule if it means I get to spend more time with you. Do you think you could be okay with me hunkered down in my studio for days on end, my focus completely on the piece I'm working on?"

She smiles. "Could I come watch you while you work? I promise to stay quiet and not distract you."

My heart snags at the thought of her in my studio. "Of course. I'd like that. Though I don't see how you being near me wouldn't be distracting." I hold up a hand to halt her retort. "You're distracting in a good way."

She blushes. "You're also distracting in a good way."

I grin. This conversation has turned out much better than I expected. "That's nice to hear."

I lean forward, and she meets me halfway for another mind-blowing kiss. When we pull away, Abbie covers her mouth with a hand, but I hear her yawn.

"You're right, it's late and we've had a busy weekend. As much as I'd like to stay here, we both need a good night's sleep before work tomorrow."

Abbie tenses in my arms, and she gets a panicked look on her face. She groans. "I'd forgotten all about work for a minute. I'm so nervous about the meeting tomorrow."

I rub circles on her back, hoping she finds it somewhat soothing. "Whatever happens, you'll be okay. You're Abbie Price. You'll figure out a game plan and execute it to perfection."

Her mouth curves up slightly on one side, but worry lines still etch her forehead. I reach up and try to smooth them away with my thumb. "Thanks for the vote of confidence, Carlos. We'll see what happens, I guess."

I wish I could erase her anxiety. "Can I call you tomorrow after school gets out to find out what happens?"

She nods. "I'd like that."

I move Abbie from my lap to the cushion next to me, then

pull out my phone and order a ride share before handing her my keys. "Are you going to be able to drive with your sprained ankle?"

"I'll put it in a boot and it will be fine. Besides, it's my left ankle, not my driving foot."

"You just happen to have a boot lying around your apartment?"

She grins. "You'd be surprised how many medical supplies I keep on hand."

"What? Miss Scout is over prepared? I'm shocked."

Abbie laughs, and it's such a melodious sound in my ears.

"I guess I'll go home and crash. Is there anything I can do for you before I go?"

She shakes her head. "You've done more than enough. I'll be fine."

I give her a hug and a kiss before standing up. "Okay, if you're sure. I'll see myself out."

Not wanting to press my luck, but unable to resist the sweet smile on her face, I lean down for one more kiss before I go. When I stick my hand in my pocket, my fingers hit something solid and smooth.

"I almost forgot," I say, closing my fingers around the object. "I wanted to give you this."

Removing my hand, I hold it in front of Abbie, opening my fingers to reveal the contents. She stares at the glass pendant for a bit before taking it from my palm.

"It's so pretty," she says, her voice breathy.

"It reminds me of your eyes."

She pulls my arm while raising her chin, and I lean down for a lingering kiss, which only ends when my phone buzzes in my pocket. I pull it out and read the message, then sigh. "My ride's here."

Abbie frowns, but still has a hold on my arm and it takes three more kisses before she finally lets go. The only reason I'm able to walk out the door is the promise that we'll see each other again soon.

31

Abbie

I DID NOT sleep well. After Carlos left, my mind alternated between the potential outcomes of my meeting with Will and Human Resources this morning and replaying the events of the past two days. Carlos texted me this morning, wishing me luck at work. I have a feeling I'm really going to enjoy whatever's happening between us.

Carlos likes me. And I like him, which probably surprised us both. I cannot wait to see Rachel's expression when I tell her about the weekend. I'm sure she'll be thrilled. And now I don't have to be a third wheel to her and Tom or a fifth wheel when Julie and Jayson join us. Though, I'm sure Julie will have something to say about all of this after I tried to warn her off of Jayson because he was friends with Carlos. Oh well. I'll endure it. Because I now like Carlos. The thought warms me from head to toe.

My mood sours as I drive onto campus. I'm jittery with

nerves, scared that today's the day I get fired. I can't think of a single credible reason Will might have for dismissing me because I'm great at my job. I'd be even better if Will would let me loose to run the summer clinic I know would benefit both the university and local high school students. At least I'll know what kept me up half the night in about thirty minutes.

I park Carlos's truck and head up to my office. I probably should have brought a cardboard box just in case, but I didn't want to jinx myself. I'm sure HR has a whole stack of them for when they're needed. I make some calls and run through my daily schedule with the intention of still having a job after this meeting.

The alarm on my phone goes off, giving me a five minute warning. Might as well be early for once and shake things up. I walk down to Will's office and knock. The door opens, and it's a man I don't recognize.

"You must be Abigail Price."

He motions me in and I see Will sitting at his desk.

"You can just call me Abbie."

He nods. "Abbie it is. I'm Travis Childers. Nice necklace."

Instinctively, I touch the glass pendant. I found a leather cord in my kitchen's miscellany drawer that the pendant loop fit perfectly on. It feels sort of like Carlos is with me for whatever I'm facing this morning, and I really need someone in my corner right now.

"Thanks," I say. "Nice to meet you." I'm not really thrilled to be meeting with HR, but I was raised to be polite.

"What happened to your foot?"

I appreciate his observation skills. I bet Will wouldn't have said anything. Of course, being observant is probably something you learn in HR training. "Just a sprained ankle. It'll be right as rain in no time."

Will motions me to the three empty chairs in front of his desk.

"Have a seat. Faye Danvers from HR will be here shortly."

My brow furrows. I don't like the idea of us needing two people from HR for this discussion. Hopefully, whatever the reason for dismissal, it won't keep me from finding another AT position. I don't know what else I'd do if I couldn't work with student athletes.

I pick the seat to the right and Travis sits in the one next to me. He and Will chat about the various sports programs at UNCA while I try to keep my breathing even. It would not bode well if I had a panic attack right now. My fingers rub the smooth glass of the pendant, which calms me a little.

There's a knock at the door and a woman who looks vaguely familiar enters. She must be Faye. "Sorry I'm late. Let's get started."

Will nods and turns to me. "Abigail, I know we haven't always seen eye to eye and I've been known to micromanage a bit."

That's the understatement of the year, but I keep my facial expression neutral.

"You've been doing wonderful with the basketball team," he continues. "I've gotten nothing but high praise from the players and coaching staff."

This pleases me, but I only nod. I'm mentally preparing myself for my termination, so his next words come as a complete shock.

"I've decided to retire. Travis here is going to be our new Athletics Director, starting next month. I thought you two should meet while he's here for a visit."

My eyebrows shoot to the sky. Will's leaving after such a short time? This seems really sudden. Could it be a health issue?

Even though we've clashed, I don't wish him any harm. Of course, I don't know him well enough to ask questions. "Oh, okay."

I smile at my future boss, but it probably looks stiff because I'm feeling thrown off. I wonder if he'd be open to my summer clinic. Almost as if he can hear my thoughts, he smiles and nods. I laugh inwardly, hoping this is a premonition of good things to come.

"I've heard many wonderful things about you, Abbie," Travis says. "I look forward to working with you. We'll have an official meeting next month when I take over to sit down and discuss your work and what you might need from me. I'm very interested to hear any ideas you may have for the athletic training program."

"That sounds great. I do have some thoughts on training schedules and protocols that could benefit the program." I'm still feeling a little dazed. "Can I ask why HR is here?"

"We haven't officially announced my retirement," Will says, "so everything said here has to be kept quiet for a couple of weeks. Faye's here to verify that everyone knows and understands the situation."

I nod slowly. "Ah, okay. Is there anything else?"

"No, that's it. Thanks for coming in."

Travis extends his hand when I stand up. "So great to meet you, Abbie. I can't wait to hear your ideas."

I shake his hand and smile, thrilled by the fact that I will soon have a boss who values my input about the program. When I return to my office, I slump into my chair, relieved that I still have my job. That was an interesting few minutes. I can't wait to tell Carlos.

My smile widens at the thought. He's going to be ecstatic to hear that the meeting wasn't anything major. I send him a quick text in case he's been worrying about it like me. He sends back a party horn with confetti and I chuckle. I love his enthusiasm and support. He's so wonderful. I'm glad we dealt with the past because now it means there's room for a future. I can't wait to see where it goes.

Epilogue

Fifteen Months Later

Abbie

IT'S HOT, AND my back is a river of sweat. Carlos and I are hiking to one of his favorite waterfalls, one we haven't been to together yet. The trail is long and steep in a few points. It's a gorgeous, cloudless day, but the sun and humidity are adding to the exertion of our trek.

"Can we stop for some water?"

Carlos turns back to face me. "Sure, Socks. It's only a couple hundred more yards, I think. Once we get up these stairs, we'll be there."

I look past him at the terrain, ignoring his favorite nickname for me. Secretly, I love it, but no self-respecting person would ever admit to enjoying being called an item of clothing. His "stairs" are foot high indentions in the side of the mountain. "Great."

I pull the bottle out of the pocket of my backpack and guzzle the water greedily. I wipe my chin to get rid of the water that dribbled out of the sides of my mouth and hold the bottle out. "Would you like some?"

"Yes, thank you." He smiles and his eyes crinkle at the corners. My insides flutter with the way he's looking at me. I don't think I'll ever tire of his loving gazes.

He returns the water bottle, and I tuck it back into its place. I straighten up and square my shoulders. "Okay, I'm ready. Lead on."

Carlos reaches out, takes my hand, and helps me up the steep terrain. He's such an amazing man. It's almost hard to believe I ever hated him. He's been so sweet with my nephew, CJ. He'll make a great father someday. I'm sure Rachel's tired of me dropping in to check in on the newest member of the family so much. Though Carlos and I have babysat plenty to give her and Tom time together so she can't complain too much.

The new AD has been a breath of fresh air. He's given me free rein on my schedule, agreed to the summer clinic, which went phenomenally last summer, and seems pleased with how things are going. The basketball team won the conference and made it into the NCAA tournament again last year without Marcus Cobb, who ended up transferring to NC State. Most of the players are returning this year, so there's hope for a repeat trip to the tournament next spring.

We crest the hill and the waterfall appears in front of us. I rest my arms on the guardrail and stare, mesmerized by the large flow of water. The droplets coming off the falls shimmer in the sun, demonstrating why this is called Rainbow Falls.

"Carlos, this is amazing. I can see why it's one of your favorites."

He smiles, though this time it doesn't reach his eyes. He seems a little off from his normal, carefree self today. I wonder if he's stressing about his latest commission work. He's had a steady stream of customers over the past year. His work was featured in one of the Amazing Asheville ads we shot and his art has been a hot commodity ever since. He's supposed to have a gallery show in a few months and has been working on pieces for that as well. Even though he no longer works at the elementary school, I've hardly seen him recently unless I venture out to his studio. But I understand. When the season gets underway in a few months, I'll be just as busy as he is.

It's the reason I'm treasuring our hike today. I know he should be in the studio, but he is very purposeful about making sure we get quality time together regularly.

"This view is great, but if we walk a little farther, we can get down closer to the waterfall and feel the spray. It'd be a great opportunity to cool off. You look a little pink."

He's being kind. I know my face probably resembles a ripe tomato. "Sure."

He links our hands and we walk downhill for a few yards before taking a sharp left that leads us down to a small viewing area about halfway down the falls. The mist hits my face and I feel immediate relief from the heat. I close my eyes and take a minute to enjoy the cooling effect.

I open them just in time to see the sun hit the water and create a vibrant rainbow. The beauty is stunning. I reach out for Carlos, not wanting to look away. "Carlos, are you seeing this?"

"Beautiful."

I nod. "It sure is."

"I'm not talking about the falls. I'm talking about you."

I scoff and turn toward him, ready to argue. "Come on, now.

I look like—"

The words die on my tongue when I see Carlos kneeling in front of me, a medium-sized, wrapped, rectangular box in his hand. My hands fly to my mouth. Is this what I think it is? The box is way too big for a ring, but we'd talked about this. I don't like to have anything on my hands when I'm working. I meet Carlos's gaze and the depth of emotion in them brings me to tears.

"Abbie. I knew in high school you were special. I messed up my chance then to tell you how I felt, but am grateful that Amazing Asheville brought us together again. Those two days were some of the most fun I've ever had. Every day I get to spend with you is an adventure and I hope to have many more together. You are so smart, determined, kind, tenacious, loyal, and loving."

A lump forms in my throat at his words. This is definitely what I think it is, and my heart rate is rocketing out of control. I focus on his mouth and try to hear everything he's saying so I can keep it in my heart.

"You are a warrior for those you care about, and I love knowing that you're in my corner. Thank you for all of your support and flexibility through everything that's happened with my art career. I hope you feel as cared for and supported as I do. I love you so much and want to spend the rest of my life proving that to you. Abigail Elizabeth Price, will you marry me?"

"Yes, Carlos! Yes, I'll marry you."

He stands up and wraps me in a hug, and we kiss. It's a long, slow kiss and tears track down my cheeks the entire time. I'm so happy.

I'm also curious.

"What's in the box, Carlos?"

He laughs and lets go of me. "Oh, right. Sorry. See for yourself."

He hands me the box. I carefully remove the paper, which Carlos stuffs into the open backpack at his feet. I open the lid and pull out a heavy, wrapped object. I remove the paper and am stunned to find a beautiful rainbow-hued vase in my hands. I look up at Carlos.

"Is this the vase I saw during the competition?"

"Yes."

I hug it to my chest. "I went there a couple of weeks after the competition to get it, but was told it had been sold."

Carlos chuckles. "That's not technically accurate. I saw you eying it when we were there and had Doug pull it off of the floor for me."

"Oh, Carlos, thank you! This is perfect."

Carlos reaches into his pocket and pulls out a small, square box, which he holds out to me. My mouth falls open. He gently takes the vase from me and replaces it in the box, tucking it back into his pack. He puts the smaller box in my hands.

"I see your brain working overtime, but open it and then hear me out."

I lift the lid and a gorgeous diamond solitaire ring is nestled inside. Okay, so I know I'd told him I didn't want a ring, but I really want to see what this looks like on my finger. Carlos takes the ring from the box and slides it onto my left ring finger.

"I saw this in a store window and immediately knew it'd look great on you. I know you can't really wear it while you're working, but I thought maybe you'd want to wear it whenever you're not on campus. And…" He reaches into his pocket and pulls out a delicate gold chain. "In case you wanted to keep it with you while working, I made this for you."

I choke up with emotion. The way he loves me is so incredible. I blink rapidly a few times to clear the tears from my eyes.

"Oh my gosh, Carlos. This is too much!"

"Nothing will ever be too much for you. Can I put the chain on you?"

I nod and pull my ponytail away from my neck so he can fasten it. I place a hand on it. "It's so beautiful. I'd say I can't believe you made this, but that would be a lie. You are so incredibly talented that nothing is outside your artistic wheelhouse."

"Thanks. You've become my muse."

My heart swells at his words and I can't help myself. I launch myself into his arms, kissing his lips, his cheek, forehead, nose, whatever I can reach. He wraps his arms around me, chuckling. "You're welcome, I guess."

"I love you so much, Carlos."

He squeezes me tightly against him. "I love you too."

Thank you for reading *Stuck With You*! If you enjoyed it, please consider leaving a review online.

🏆🏆🏆🏆🏆

Want to stay in the know on future books? Sign up for my newsletter at MeganByrd.net/newsletter

Find additional *Stuck With You* content including a bonus scene at MeganByrd.net/stuckwithyou

ACKNOWLEDGEMENTS

Quinton Sawyer, thank you for sharing your knowledge of the college athletic training industry and reading parts of the manuscript to ensure as much accuracy as possible. Any discrepancies or errors are mine.

My Sweet Reader Facebook Group, thank you for sharing your thoughts and enthusiasm as I worked through various cover concepts, blurbs, and character descriptions. I value your feedback.

Jeff Pittman (aka the Real Reece Skyland), thank you for inspiring me through your beautiful paintings of Asheville and the Blue Ridge Mountains (find his amazing stuff at JeffPittman.com)

Heather Gerwing, thank you for your sage advice, honest feedback, and willingness to provide detailed ideas throughout the publishing process.

Anna Booraem, thank you for your friendship and geeking out with me about the writing life (and commiserating/celebrating rejections with me).

Cali, BJ, Susie, and Chantal, thank you for Beta reading and answering my questions about early versions of the story. You definitely made Abbie and Carlos's book better! We all thank you.

Maureen Ollivant, thank you for your support and your proofreading skills!

Lioputra, thank you for the awesome character illustrations.

As always, thank you to my family for all of your love and support (Kaitlyn, thanks for letting me bounce ideas off of you). Your encouragement and kind words keep me moving forward on this journey.

ABOUT THE AUTHOR

Megan Byrd lives in Asheville, North Carolina with her husband and two kids. She hates running, but loves hiking in the mountains toward a waterfall or scenic view and taking a variety of classes including kickboxing, HIIT, yoga, and Zumba. When she's not reading, writing, or chasing waterfalls, she enjoys visiting local bookstores, wandering through thrift shops in search of special finds, listening to live music, and catching up with friends.

Want to be first to know when the next book is available? Sign up on the website to receive a monthly e-newsletter and read about behind-the-scenes sneak peeks of her current work-in-progress, book recommendations, and other fun things. You can also visit MeganByrd.net/my_books to learn more about the inspiration behind her books.

Website: MeganByrd.net
Instagram: @megan.e.byrd
Facebook: Facebook.com/authormeganbyrd
Facebook Reader Group:
Facebook.com/groups/meganbyrdsweetreaders

Made in the USA
Columbia, SC
03 May 2024